A SISTER'S PROMISE

A Thriller

James Caine

Twisted Thriller Books

Dear son,

I love you more than you currently love penguins.

Love,
Dad

PROLOGUE

I slowly open my eyes to darkness. My head pounds with a relentless dull ache. I try to move, but panic when my movement is restricted.

My memory is fuzzy. I try to remember how I got here. I try again to stand up but can't. Where am I? My body is curled up in a ball, and my head is spinning.

While I'm disoriented, I realize it's not just my head that's moving, but the space I'm trapped in as well. When I hear the honk of a car horn coming from outside the darkness, it confirms it. I'm in the trunk of a car.

I blink, hoping my eyes will adjust in the dark, but it's useless. Is this really happening or some terrible nightmare? I'm in shock and try to calm my nerves. The distant sounds of a car radio hit me, along with the muffled sounds of someone whistling to the song playing.

"Help!" I shout. "Help me! Please! My name's Sarah! Sarah Roland!" The driver turns the radio down and I call for help again.

There's a moment of silence before my calls for help are answered. "Shut up, Sarah!" the driver says, turning up the music again.

My body stiffens as I remember everything. I know

exactly how I got here and who did this to me. I even have a clue as to where I'm being brought to. It's the same place the murderer brought their last victim.

As reality hits me, I begin to scream. The driver turns the radio to maximum and begins whistling again.

As the pain in my head increases, I feel the urge to close my eyes again. I try my best to fight it but can't win.

"Sarah!" a voice calls out to me in the darkness.

It wasn't the driver who said my name this time. It was someone else. A familiar voice, but it's too dark to see anything. The trunk is too small, but I know someone else is in here with me.

"Sarah!" the voice shouts.

CHAPTER 1

Sister
Before

When a loved one disappears, it's easy to think the worst.

They must be dead. They have to be. Otherwise, they wouldn't be missing.

I've been dealing with my emotions all week. I cry, get angry, and even just stare blankly. Sometimes I feel like I'm not even inside my own body.

What happened to him? Where is he? Is he alive? Dead?

I try not to let my imagination run with what could be happening to him if he is alive. Knowing my brother, this could all be part of some stupid joke.

Mickey's done many stupid things in the past, but that would take the cake. How old is he? Of course, I know the answer. He's my twin. Ironically, we weren't born on the same day, though. I came first at 11:59 pm, followed by Mickey minutes later.

Ironic is how you could describe Mickey and me as well. Mickey was a fun-loving jokester, while I was more serious. He would always poke fun at how studious I was or how much effort I put into everything in my life. He was a coaster. Got by with doing the bare minimum.

That was us in a nutshell. The Roland twins. Mickey the adventurous troublemaker, and Sarah, me, the one with the stick stuck up her butt, as Mickey would put it.

I smile, thinking about how annoying Mickey can be while being the funniest person at the same time. Somehow his humor makes him charming. Or rather, it *made* him charming.

I remind myself to stop thinking the worst, but it's so hard not to.

Mickey's gone.

It's been almost a week. Police believe he left town.

Part of me wonders if he's on his way to see me. I left Pinewood Springs years ago, while Mickey stayed behind. It was something we fought about often.

I moved across the country to Toronto for school while he stayed in small-town Alberta.

I knew he resented me for leaving. I resent myself sometimes after what happened. I couldn't stay though. I couldn't stand to watch another day of my mother deteriorating slowly in front of me. She was sick with cancer for most of my teenage years. Soon after Mickey and I turned twenty, the cancer got much worse. Things were not looking well, but she kept fighting. She stayed alive.

Mickey would joke that I got my stubbornness from Mom. She refused to let her sickness win. When he said that to me when I was younger, I was annoyed, but now I take it as a badge of honor.

My mom fought her cancer for years and wouldn't give up.

I hate myself for thinking she should have. Would it have been easier for her, and Mickey and me, if she just peacefully passed? Sure, I got more time with her, but knowing how the eventual end for her was coming, it was unbearable.

I decided to leave. I left town, my mother and brother.

Mom wouldn't be by herself though. She remarried six years ago to John. He owned a hardware store in town. The two met when Mom needed to buy some floor tiles and John gave her a discount. The next day he showed up at our door with flowers for her.

I didn't know what to think of John at first when he entered the picture. After they married, he said it would be okay if I wanted to call him "Dad", but I refused. I never knew my real father and didn't need a replacement. I was too old to care about having a father figure in my life.

Thankfully, John is a decent man. Otherwise, I'm not sure I could have left Palmwood Springs. Mickey was not the type to care for Mom on his own. I don't believe he was capable of doing so.

I wouldn't be.

Sometimes I wonder though what things would have been like for Mickey had he left town as well. Would he still have gone down the terrible road he took?

I look on my phone and search for flights back to Alberta. Thankfully my professors at university are giving me some time off, but I'm not sure how much more I can take without it impacting my semester.

I'm in my senior year as a criminology student at the University of Toronto. Only one more year until adulthood truly starts. Thankfully, I picked a degree that will open many doors and be worth the dollars I spent for tuition. I can be a criminologist someday... Truthfully, I'm not sure what I had in mind when I took criminology.

There's plenty of majors I could have taken that would have guaranteed me a job with good pay, and mine is not one of them.

I wanted to leave Palmwood Springs as soon as I could so I'm not sure how much thought I put into what I wanted to take. Criminology just seemed so interesting.

I search through multiple sites to find the best price to bring me back to my hometown. I'm not sure why I'm doing this. Even if I go back to Pinewood Springs, what can I do to find Mickey?

He's become a totally different person to the brother I knew. He's no longer the same. Soon after I left, and Mother got worse, he found a new way to deal with his emotions.

Drugs. The hard type. The kind of drugs that people don't advertise on t-shirts and celebrate on 4/20.

He's changed. New friends. A new girlfriend. Judging from what I can see on Facebook, she seems like a piece of work too. Jenn Harring is her name. Despite Mickey being missing, she doesn't seem to care when I search on her social media.

Snooping on his girlfriend's Facebook, she only had one post about my brother. "Miss you," is all she wrote. It had three likes and one heart emoji attached to it. One commenter asked if they'd found him yet.

The answer was no.

My cell buzzes. I stare at the screen and see the call is from my stepfather, John. I'm reluctant to pick it up. This has to be about Mickey. It must be. An update of some kind.

My stomach turns as I think about what John might tell me. I remind myself to stop thinking so negative. Maybe I'm just pessimistic, or perhaps I'm being realistic.

It could even be the twin connection people joked about Mickey and I having.

My gut is telling me the worst about what happened to my brother.

When my phone buzzes a fifth time, I take the call. "Hey, John," I say. I don't let him beat around the bush. I need to know if what I fear is true. "Do you have an update on Mickey?"

CHAPTER 2

Brother

I walk into the bedroom and see my sister sitting on a bed. She's covering her face, attempting to hide her tears poorly. Her body trembles when I try to console her.

"It's okay, Sarah," I say. She doesn't respond. I lower my head, trying to find the right words to say, not that it matters.

My sister's wearing a slim black dress that fits her well. I remember when we were kids, and she had a little weight to her, I would tease her. I was the thin twin for a long time. When Mom got sick, Sarah lost most of the extra weight she carried.

I know I could be a mean brother at times, but isn't that what brothers do? Annoy their siblings? Since everything happened, I can't stop thinking about what things were like when we were kids together.

Sarah lowers her hand and gently places them on the bed sheets. She suddenly shakes her head. "This is hard, Mickey," she says softly. Her words hit me. I wish I could do or say something that would make things easier. Instead, I watch as she tries to collect herself. "This is a hard day."

I nod, trying to find the words to calm her. "I know,

Sarah. I know."

A knock on the door gets Sarah's attention. I stand to the side of the room as my sister walks past me and opens the door.

"Hey," John says in a hushed voice. He's dressed in black as well. My stepfather was always a handsome man, but in his sharp suit and greying hair, I can see why my mother was infatuated with him.

John steps into the bedroom. "How are you managing?" he asks my sister, ignoring me. I'm used to it now.

Sarah nods. "I'm ready to get this over with," she says with an anxious laugh. She stands up from the bed and gives John a thin smile. It suddenly vanishes as she covers her face and more tears come.

My heart aches as I watch her. John wraps his arms around my sister. "I know," he says. "I miss him too."

Sarah shakes her head. "I should have been here. I should have never left town."

John takes a deep breath. "You did what was right for you, Sarah. Don't think your family would ever think otherwise. University is important."

She wipes her tears with her hand. "Not as important as my family. I wish—"

"It's okay, Sarah," I tell her. I reach out to touch my sister's shoulder but retract my hand as John holds her again.

"We'll get through this," he says, "okay? Ready to leave?"

Sarah nods reluctantly. "Let's go."

John sighs. "Melanie's having a bad day," he says. "Alice is going to stay with her. So she may not come."

"It's okay," Sarah says. "Melanie doesn't understand

it all." She smiles. "Melanie asked me this morning when she'll see him again. She asked when he'll wake up." She lets out a laugh. "Sometimes I wish I could see the world her way."

John smiles back. "She can make difficult times easier sometimes. I'll wait by the front door for you." He leaves the room.

Sarah fixes her dress and takes another deep breath. "I can do this," she whispers.

"I'm here, Sarah," I tell her. "I'll help you get through this, okay?"

She looks around the room, and suddenly our eyes meet. She doesn't say a word to me, though. Sarah lowers her head before leaving the room.

I follow slowly behind her.

The car ride to the cemetery is quiet. No one says a word. Every now and then I hear a soft whimper coming from Sarah in the front seat. At one point John softly rubs the top of her shoulder, but doesn't say a word.

I don't either. What can you say to make this an easier day? Typically, I'd crack a joke or say something stupid at my expense just to lift our spirits. This is the hardest day of my life, though. I can't even find the energy to make light of things.

I follow my stepfather and sister through the cemetery. They stop in front of a small gathering. Several friends and family members are at the burial site. My uncle from my mom's side is smoking a large cigar, talking to my aunt.

I'm surprised by how small the gathering is, but I shouldn't be.

What does shock me is seeing Jenn here. My ex-girlfriend is wearing dark, thick sunglasses and a slender dress. The dress doesn't fit her well. I wonder how old it is. It looks like it's meant to be worn by someone twenty pounds heavier.

Behind her are my two friends, Jake Matthews and Lenny Mercer. They are the type to stand out in any crowd. Both are over six feet and tower over many in Pinewood Springs. The pair could be easily mistaken for wrestlers.

Jake's wearing a muscle shirt revealing his bulging arms. Lenny is smoking a cigarette and when he finishes, he tosses the butt behind him.

Sarah notices all three of them. She glances at John, and he gives her a stern look. "I know," he says. "Not here."

Sarah nods; she looks over at Lenny who's whispering something to Jake. The pair laugh.

Embarrassed is an understatement at how my own friends are making me feel at the moment. It's a funeral. What are you doing? Show some respect. I don't say anything, though. I keep my mouth shut. I'm known for making scenes, but I won't today.

I'll keep my composure. I promised myself I would. I promised Sarah as well that I would be a better brother to her, as best I can, especially today.

Lenny and Jake's laughter dies down as the casket begins to lower into the ground. Once it's at the bottom, my ex-girlfriend and friends leave. I stand beside Sarah and John and look down at the large hole where the casket is. The three of us stand in silence.

After some time, John wipes his eyes and pats Sarah on the back. "I'll be in the car. Take your time."

Sarah nods without looking away from the tombstone. When we're alone, my sister finally breaks the silence.

"Why, Mickey?" she asks.

I lower my head. "What do you mean?"

"Why couldn't you get your act together?" she says, raising her voice slightly. She looks around the cemetery to confirm we're alone. She shakes her head. "Why were you so stupid!?"

"Sis," I say, trying to calm her.

What can I say? I messed up. I always do. I'm always the failure in the family. Sarah was the golden child, and I was the screwed-up one. Destined to be where I am today.

"Why couldn't you get your life together?" Sarah says through gritted teeth. She looks down at the casket. Tears begin to well up. Her facial expression changes from sad to angry.

"I tried," I say.

I'm not sure if that's true though. I was destined to fail at every attempt to better myself. How many times had I promised to turn things around? I even promised on my mother's grave that I would, but those words were empty.

"Who did this to you?" Sarah asks.

I don't answer. Instead, I look down at the casket with Sarah. As more tears form in her eyes, I reach out to her. My hand meets hers for a moment until it slips through her, like air. I take a step back at my inability to help her.

Sarah turns to me, but looks straight through me. She wipes her eyes and gazes at the tombstone. "Who did this to you?" she cries.

The two of us stand in silence as we look at my tombstone. My supposed final resting place.

CHAPTER 3

Brother

The worst part about being dead is not knowing how you died.

I'm not in pain. I don't get hungry or tired.

The worst part of me, my addiction, is no longer a factor anymore. I feel so clear in my mind. I feel like myself again.

The fears and worries that drove me to my addiction have emptied out of my heart.

That is if I have a heart.

I'm not sure what I am anymore. I used to enjoy watching scary movies about ghosts and ghouls. I thought about what happens when you die. This is not what I expected.

For someone who's dead, I feel like I have so much energy. I feel like that's what I might be, pure energy at its core.

I can't walk through walls, though. As far as I know, I can't haunt people either. Scare them by moving chairs across floors. If I could, I wonder if the less mature side of me would go back to my stepfather's house and continuously hide his keys from him just for fun.

I was fully aware that I was deceased before we came

to the cemetery. It's weird but I'm not overly emotional about dying. I'm more upset over how the loss of my physical body has impacted my sister. It's been difficult seeing her so upset and not being able to comfort her.

While I may not be overemotional that I'm dead, I do get angry. What upsets me is not knowing why I'm dead or who did this to me. How did it even happen?

I quickly attempt to touch my head, but my hands pass through my own body. I remember very little about what actually happened to me.

The night I was killed, I was so full of hope. I wanted to change my life around for the better. This time I meant it, at least I think so.

Drugs had taken over my life. All I wanted was the next high. The next escape. That way I wouldn't have to think about life... and death. I wouldn't have to worry about what a screw-up I was. If I got high, I could float above all my worries.

I had overdosed a week before my death. I nearly died.

Now that I'm actually dead, I wonder if it would have been better if I died when I OD'd instead. Being murdered makes things much worse.

With a drug-related death, there's no question about why it happened. The conclusion is clear. I died because of drugs. I died from an addiction I had.

Why was I murdered? Who killed me?

They are questions I know that plague my sister as I watch her stare at my tombstone.

The night I overdosed, it was my girlfriend, Jenn, who saved me. She gave me CPR. She told me later that I wasn't breathing. She wasn't sure for how long, but it must not have been a long time.

I didn't even go to the emergency room or anything.

If I could slap the side of my head, I would right now. How stupid was I? How did I let my life go the way it had? I could still be alive. I could have gone to school, like my sister, or done something with my life. Instead, I messed it all up.

After my near-death experience, I thought a lot about my life and what I wanted. It seemed that it took me nearly dying to realize that I needed a change.

It had to start with the company I kept. My friends. Jake and Lenny. My girlfriend. I couldn't be associated with any of them anymore.

I had to walk away from them.

I remember thinking about moving out of my house. Go somewhere else. Be someone else. Move to a place where I wasn't a screw-up. I could be someone respectable. Get a steady job. A beautiful wife. Maybe even kids someday if I could get my act together.

None of that matters now, of course.

After the overdose, I knew I couldn't stay in Pinewood Springs any longer. I couldn't stay in my house. Too many bad memories.

After my mother passed away, my sister and I inherited our family home.

John agreed to move out and buy his own house. In hindsight, I wonder what it would have been like had he stayed in our family home. I wonder if I would have spiralled the way I had if another man whom I respected was living with me.

I remind myself how much I resented working for John at his hardware store. He hired me part time to help out. I realize now that it was a favor to me, but when I was alive, I treated it like I was doing him the favor.

Ugh. What a little shit I was.

I wish I could have the clear mind I have now in the body that used to belong to me.

Now I want to know who took that body away from me. Is that why I'm still here?

Why am I here?

What's the purpose of this? It's agonizing watching Sarah today. Mom's gone. Now me. I wonder what she's thinking now?

The night I died, I officially broke things off with Jenn. She cried and tried to get me to take her back, but I refused. After she left my house, I remember looking around and wanting to get into my car and leave. Leave this town behind. Hit the road. Start my new life right away. I didn't want to be here anymore.

I thought about flushing my stash of drugs. In fact, I think I was about to when the picture in my living room of my mother, Sarah and me caught my attention. It's a picture John took of us in that same room. Almost everything in the picture was still the same. I had the same couch. Same table. I even kept the antique candles and a lamp Sarah and I bought Mom.

Almost everything in that photo was still in the living room, except my mother, who had passed, and my sister, who'd moved.

The smiles on the three of our faces made me pause.

I took out my phone and called Sarah that night. I was so upset when she didn't pick up. I wanted to tell her my plan.

When her voicemail beeped, I left a message instead.

"Hey, sis," I said. "it's your little bro. I know things have been hard lately with us... but I want that to change. I sort of need your help, though. Call me back when you get this."

I couldn't stay in this house anymore. If I did, I'd revert back to the old me. I needed a change. Maybe I could stay on her couch a few nights to sort out my life.

I was ready for change, I knew. I smiled as I looked at our family picture. I turned up my speakers and played one of my favorite songs that I enjoyed listening to when I was in a good mood. Embarrassingly, it was *We Are the Champions* by Queen. It may be an oldie, but there was something about that chorus that made me feel like I was on top of the world, and that night, for a brief moment, I was.

Then I felt a thump to the back of my head. My eyes closed and my body went limp.

When I opened my eyes, I knew I was dead.

Sarah takes a deep breath and starts to walk away from my tombstone, only she's not going in the direction of my stepfather's car.

"Where are we going now, Sarah?" I ask. She doesn't respond, of course.

Tears are welling up in her eyes again and I wish I could make them stop. It's because of me that she's torn up inside. There's nothing I can do besides watch.

As we continue to walk through the cemetery, it dawns on me where we're heading. I haven't been to visit in a long time. I was so preoccupied with my own disaster of a life to see her.

I had wondered before we came to the cemetery if I'd see others like me. More people who are detached from their physical bodies.

I haven't, though.

Part of me wishes I could, just to have someone to actually talk to.

I had also wished that I could see *her* again. I always thought that when you died, you'd be able to see your loved ones who passed.

Instead, it's just me.

Sarah stops in front of a different tombstone.

"Hey, Mom," she says in a hushed voice.

CHAPTER 4

Sister

I stare blankly at the stone in front of me. I prepare myself for more tears as I read her name.

Angela Berthume.

My mom. She died too young. She died knowing she was going to die. She had battled breast cancer for years, giving Mickey and me hope that she'd win. We should have known better.

When I went to her funeral, she looked nothing like the woman who mothered me. She had lost such a tremendous amount of weight that she looked unnatural. I almost felt that the woman in the casket was an imposter.

I resented myself for leaving Pinewood Springs years ago. I couldn't take it. I had to leave. If I'd stayed, my life would have been on pause until she died.

I hated myself for even thinking that way.

I should have stayed. Her only daughter, and I left her.

I take a deep breath as tears well up from deep inside me. I remind myself that my mother wasn't alone. She had her husband, John. He stayed by her side as she withered away. I can't imagine how difficult that would be.

Soon after they got married, we found out about Mom's cancer. Nearly the entire time they were together, she had her diagnosis.

Mom had Mickey too. For all his faults, my brother had a way to lighten any tough situation. I can't help but smile as I think about the jokes he'd play when Mom was struggling, just to get a smile on her face.

I let out a laugh now as I think of it.

Mickey was a different person back then. Sure, he was using drugs, but not any type of substance that society hadn't accepted.

We all didn't mind his pot use, even though it was pretty extensive. Mickey tried to encourage Mom to try some, saying that his friends told him it was better than the cancer drugs she had been taking for years.

She declined him but thought the gesture came from a good place.

As I think about what Mickey became, a flash of rage hits me.

"Why were you so stupid, Mickey?" I say to myself. "Why? Why!"

Ever since I arrived back in town, and after knowing the fate of my brother, my emotions have been all over the place. I'll switch from sadness to anger, or rage to peace. Contempt to just wanting to scream until I lose my voice.

I know it's part of the grieving process. I know that. It doesn't make it easier. I feel like a lunatic as I switch between emotions every minute.

If my brother took some responsibility, none of this would have happened. Had he once followed through with his promises to get off the drugs, he wouldn't be six feet under.

"You're so stupid," I mutter under my breath. "I hate you for this. I hate you."

As my blood continues to boil, I feel a warm sensation come over me. A sense of calmness like a comforting blanket.

I relax my tense shoulders and unclench my fist. It's almost like the anger flowing inside me hits a red light and a green glow of peace comes over me.

Suddenly, I'm not as angry anymore.

Memories of when I was younger flow through my mind now.

We never knew our biological father. He left town before we turned three. But that didn't stop Mickey and I from having love in our house. Our mom worked double time to ensure that.

My parents never married. They never got along either. Mom rarely talked of our biological father. He was not a part of my life or Mickey's.

As much as I first hated John when he started dating my mom, he wasn't a bad guy. He could come off a little pushy at times, but he loved my mom. I will forever be grateful for him for being with my mom until her last breath.

I thought it was weird that only after a year from my mom's death he was already engaged to Alice. I couldn't help but wonder if he had something going on with her while my mother was still alive. Perhaps he too was having difficulties with Mom dying, that he wanted his own escape and found it with Alice.

Alice was a friend of my mom's as well, only making things more awkward. I don't think they were too close, though, but that's how John and her initially met, through my mom. This was Alice's second marriage as well.

Her first marriage ended in a messy divorce where Alice received full custody of her eleven-year-old daughter, Melanie.

I never really had much of a conversation with her daughter until I stayed at John's house. I knew she had an intellectual disability. She attended a special day program at a school. Alice had her hands full giving her a lot of activities to do during the week. She had swimming lessons, piano lessons, drumming circles. Alice, her devoted mother, took her everywhere.

When John called me about the news with Mickey, he offered to pick me up at the airport and let me stay with him.

Despite my reluctance, John and his new family have treated me well. When I think of the word *family*, suddenly my eyes begin to tear again.

Family. Mine is all gone now.

I finally manage to look at my mother's tombstone. "I love you, Mom. I miss you." I take a deep breath before I turn and head back towards the parking lot where my stepfather's waiting. "I love you too, Mickey," I say to myself as I head towards the car.

As I look out to the parking lot, I see three people talking. I immediately recognize them from the funeral. Mickey's girlfriend and two of his friends.

My soft features harden as I watch them talking amongst themselves. One of the men is laughing.

What could be so funny? They were giggling before his casket was lowered as well.

Did the three of them find it funny that my brother was dead?

The police believe it was a targeted attack. Someone

who likely thought Mickey had some money or drugs hanging around the large house he owned that used to belong to our mother. When they broke in, Mickey was there and must have put up a fight, leading to his death. That's what the police think.

I feel differently.

From what I know, Mickey had many blows to his head. To me that didn't come off like a stranger. Mickey knew his killer. This was personal.

Mickey left me a message the day police believe he was murdered. He asked for help.

I wished I'd picked up the phone. I wonder what he was going to ask for. Did he know he was in danger?

I may not have been able to help him when he was alive, but I can still do something for him now. I clench my fist as I watch his friends and girlfriend talk together.

I wonder if it was one of these three who killed Mickey.

I let out a breath. I'm going to figure out who did this to you, brother. I will.

CHAPTER 5
Sister

As I get closer to the parking lot, one of the men notices me.

The two men wave at Mickey's girlfriend and step into a red truck. Strangely, Jenn doesn't go with them. She lights up a cigarette and looks at the truck as it leaves the cemetery gates.

There's more to what happened with my brother. If I'm going to find out, I need to talk to the right people and get to know what my brother was really like these past few years. Who better than his on again, off again girlfriend?

I notice John sitting in his car. When he sees me, he starts the ignition. I'm not ready to leave, though.

As I pass her, she gives me a thin smile. I stop and give her a shy wave.

"I think you must be Jenn," I say. "Jenn Harring, right?"

She nods, blowing out smoke from the side of her mouth. "That's me." Now that I'm up close, I see that her eyes are red and a tear is welling in her eye. She quickly wipes it and tosses the cigarette into the parking lot. She puts out her hand. "You're Sarah," she says. I shake her hand. "Mickey's shown me pictures of you. I feel strangely like I know you even though we've never met."

"Mickey wasn't really the type to share pictures," I say, shaking my head. "I only knew what you look like from social media."

Jenn scoffs. "Typical Mickey, wasn't it?"

"Typical Mickey," I agree.

There's an awkward pause in the conversation as both of us have no clue what to say next.

"Mickey told me a lot of good things about you," she says. "You're in university in Toronto, right?"

I nod. "Their criminology program."

She makes a face. "Sounds interesting."

"Sometimes," I say.

I look out into the field of tombstones and know that two of them belong to my family. Sometimes I wonder what it would have been like had I stayed here. I take a deep breath, letting my own thoughts hit me. Sure, Mom would still have died from cancer, but maybe there was a chance that Mickey could have gone down a different road.

I can feel my stomach turn at the thought that my presence could have saved him. If it wasn't for me leaving, he could still be here.

I give a thin smile towards Jenn. "I feel terrible saying this, but I'm not even sure what Mickey was like before he —"

Jenn takes a deep breath. "You two didn't talk?" she asks. I shake my head. "That's so weird, Mickey talked about you so much that I assumed he was... or had." She scratches her face and whimpers, but I notice no tears come from her eyes. When I don't say anything, she looks at me strangely. I quickly snap out of it.

"This isn't an easy day for anyone who loves Mickey," I say.

She nods. "It is not," she agrees.

"When did you last see Mickey?" I ask, getting to the question I really wanted to ask since approaching her.

She shrugs. "It was the day before he went missing, I think. We were just hanging out at his place, watching a movie."

I nod and bite my lip. I'm sure that meant they were getting high together.

I look over at John. When he notices me, he quickly glances away.

"Do you need a ride?" I ask. "I'm sure my stepfather wouldn't mind driving you somewhere. Pinewood Springs is not huge after all." I give her a thin smile again. The more time I have with Jenn, the more I get to know not only what her relationship was like with my brother, but others in his orbit before he died.

No, before he was murdered, I remind myself.

As I stare at the light blue eyes of my brother's girlfriend, I remind myself as well that she could be involved. She may put on a pleasant face for his funeral, but whenever something terrible happens, the partner of the deceased is always a main suspect.

If watching enough Discovery Channel investigations has taught me anything, it's that.

Jenn looks over my shoulder at John sitting in his car. She quickly looks away and meets my eyes. "No, I'm fine," she says. "I called an Uber already. No buses run to the cemetery, unfortunately."

I nod. "Well, it was nice to meet you," I tell her.

"I wish it was during better times," she says, meeting my gaze.

As I get into John's car, and we begin to leave the parking lot, I look into the side mirror, watching Jenn as she gets smaller and smaller until she's out of sight.

I'm not sure what I was hoping to get from a conversation with Jenn, but I didn't find it. She says she didn't see him the day he disappeared. If only I had more time to draw it out from her, I could try and piece together what happened.

It's odd, though. While I spoke with Jenn, it was as if a voice inside me was screaming that she isn't to be trusted, but I can't explain why.

CHAPTER 6

Brother

"She's lying!" I shout in the backseat of the car. "Jenn's lying!" Of course no one can hear me, but it doesn't stop me from being completely outraged after listening to the exchange Sarah and my ex-girlfriend had.

Yes, we had a movie date at my place the day before my death, but she absolutely saw me the day I died. I broke up with her! It was soon after that I was killed.

How can Jenn say otherwise? What is she hiding?

I scoff loudly in the backseat, but nobody notices. "Really, Jenn?" I attempt to touch Sarah's shoulder in the front seat, but my hand goes through her. "You have to hear me, Sarah!" I shout. "Jenn is lying!"

Sarah continues to stare blankly out the window; I roll my eyes and sit back in the seat. "I give up!"

John turns to Sarah. "How are you doing?" he asks.

My sister nods. "As best I can, I suppose." She turns to him. "Do you know his girlfriend?"

John nods. "I wouldn't call it well, but I do know of her. They've dated more times and broken up than I have fingers and toes. Michael would tell me about it when he worked at the store."

"I hate it when you call me Michael," I say to my

stepfather. He knows that too.

I prefer Mickey. The only person allowed to call me Michael was the woman who gave birth to me. She has sole rights to do so, given the fact that she pushed me out of her.

Sarah gives a thin smile. "He hated it when you called him Michael," she says. She looks out the window again.

John smiles back. He quickly glances at her and back at the road. "Yes, he did. I guess I got used to it from your mother."

"What about his two friends?" Sarah asks him. "I knew Mickey had new friends, but I never met either of those guys. Do you know them?"

John shakes his head as he drives. "Not really."

Sarah lets out a heavy breath. "Do you know what Mickey was up to the day he disappeared?"

John continues to stare out the road, his smile fading. "No, I don't." He pauses before he continues. "He was supposed to work the day after at the store. When he didn't show up, I didn't necessarily think the worst, I admit. I just assumed he ditched his shift. That wasn't exactly uncommon."

Sarah shakes her head and looks back out the window. "I don't know why he was so difficult."

When she says the words, I slump in the chair. I know. I'm a screw-up. I get it.

John nods. "I wish it wasn't this way either. Sometimes I think that no matter what happened, had it been his disappearance or something else, we would have wound up in that cemetery for him sooner or later."

Sarah gives John a nasty stare and quickly looks away. "It wasn't a disappearance. He didn't just vanish and die, John. Someone killed him. Someone who knew him."

"Knew him," John repeats. "Police think it was a robbery."

"Police didn't know my brother," Sarah says.

"Did you?" John says, raising an eyebrow as he looks at Sarah. "Did you really know him? Did any of us at the end, really know Michael... sorry, Mickey?"

Sarah looks out the window again. "I'm not sure."

I sit up in the chair and try to pat my sister's shoulders to get her attention. It doesn't work.

"Jenn was lying to you!" I shout. I want to sit beside her and yell it into her ear, but I know there's no point. "She's hiding something," I say softly. I shake my head in disbelief. "Jenn," I scoff. "It must have been her. She actually did this to me."

"I don't trust her," Sarah says, breaking the tension in the car. "His girlfriend. I think she's hiding something."

I almost want to jump for joy as my sister comes to the conclusion I have. For a moment, I wonder if my sister somehow heard what I said.

Before in the cemetery as well, she was so angry talking about how I messed up my life so that it eventually brought me to my grave, and when I touched her, she softened. Her emotions changed.

I may be dead and no one can hear me, but does Sarah on some level understand? Is this some weird twin connection that can happen postmortem somehow?

I can't walk through walls. I can't haunt people or move objects.

Can I still communicate with my sister though?

CHAPTER 7

Sister

I lie in the bed in the guest bedroom of my stepfather's house, reminiscing about better times. Scrolling through old pictures on my Facebook, I have so many memories. Unfortunately, I didn't take too many of Mickey and me.

Everyone assumes twins live the same life. Have the same friends. Do the same thing. Have the same interests. Feel the same emotions.

Mickey and I were so different. The only things we had in common were our genetics and being born minutes from each other.

He had his friends and his life, and I had mine.

Most of the pictures on my profile are of me with my friends. I smile as I go past a photo of me and Bethany Coleman. She was my best friend in high school.

She moved north to Edmonton for university and is in their social work program. We stayed in touch for a little bit but as the years went by, she was difficult to keep up with.

Most of the pictures on my account though are with me and Drew Pickton. He was the first boy I fell head over heels for. My first love. My first kiss. My first... everything.

When I lived in Pinewood Springs, my whole life revolved around him.

We were inseparable.

I smile when I see a picture of us leaning against the wall in the high school gymnasium from an ancient Facebook profile picture.

We dated for nearly all of our high school years. All of my friends thought we were destined to be together forever. I was naive to think the same.

A few days after prom, he suddenly ended things with me. It was over so quickly, I barely had time to register that we were broken up.

"We need to talk," Drew said to me during one of the last days of school. I still remember how serious he looked when he said it to me. I thought something terrible had happened to him. Maybe he lost a family member or some other tragedy had occurred. I didn't have the slightest clue what he intended to do.

When we were alone, and away from the ears of our friends and others in the school hallways, he broke up with me. "We can't see each other anymore," he said. "Sorry."

That was it. No reason. No explanation. He left immediately after saying the words.

He wouldn't call me back when I tried to reach him. No texts. I even tried emailing.

I scoff as I think about how broken I was back then.

I flick past a picture of Drew and me, and finally I see one of Mickey and me. It was our graduation day. I made it on the honor roll but did not get valedictorian. I was so bummed about it. Mickey was happy just to have been able to graduate. I smile as I look at his crooked graduation hat. His fist is pumped in the air for the photo.

I laugh as I remember what Mickey said as Mom took the picture: "Prison's over!"

I take a deep breath as I make a post on my Facebook using the old picture of us. "Miss you brother," is all I write. I'm not the type to make posts like this on social media. Today, I feel like I haven't been myself, though.

I lower my phone. I will do my best not to cry again. I've cried so much that my own tears are starting to bother me.

I think of Mickey's girlfriend, Jenn. I bring the phone back to my face and search for her on Facebook. When I click on her profile, I look at the past few posts. None of them are from today. None are about Mickey.

She hasn't written anything about her boyfriend on the day of his funeral. Strange.

Maybe she's one of those people who doesn't post things on Facebook about terrible life moments. Typically, I'm not one to do that either. Posting about my brother, though, just now, it wasn't for likes or comments. Doing it made me feel closer to him even though he's gone.

I scroll through Jenn's feed. One post catches my attention immediately.

"Why are boys so complicated?" she wrote a week back.

I guess she is the type of person to post about her emotions online. Of course she had to be referencing Mickey. Mickey would be a complicated man, enough to drive anybody nuts. Jenn's post has a few likes and one comment. Some woman named Cathy. I don't know her. Cathy replied, "You deserve better."

I wonder what she meant. How did Mickey treat his girlfriend?

A knock on the door gets my attention. "Dinner's ready," John says on the other side.

I leave my phone on the bed and leave the room.

I join my stepfather, his wife and daughter at the dining table. Alice is the quintessential housewife. She always looks impeccable. Her brunette hair is dolled up perfectly. Today she's wearing a flowing yellow dress. She's a stay-at-home mother for her daughter, Melanie.

The four of us dine on the steak dinner Alice prepared. She's an excellent cook. If I lived in her house, I'd easily have twenty pounds more on me. I can see why John's gained weight since last time I saw him.

John compliments his wife for the great meal and sips on his wine.

Melanie turns to her mother and asks if she can have a taste, but Alice makes a face back. "You know the answer, young lady."

"Nineteen," Melanie says in a dull voice. I give a thin smile at their exchange. Melanie is wearing a yellow dress just like her mother.

Somehow, I know that if Alice had a set of twins, like Mickey and I, she would be the type to dress us in the same clothes as well and give us rhyming names like Rod and Todd.

The only conversation at dinner is mostly comments from Melanie. She's telling us some facts about penguins that she's learned. Of course we've heard her facts many times over. Since staying at my stepfather's house, I must have learned the same five facts about penguins.

Did you know that penguins talk to each other with not only their sounds but body movements? Did you know that penguins can live in groups of thousands?

Well, I do, thanks Melanie. She especially loves the

idea that there could be thousands of penguins in one place. One big happy family.

There's a small room beside the dining area where Melanie likes to make her crafts. Many of them center around penguins, of course.

John takes another sip of wine after clearing his throat. He's just as quiet as me. Every so often, I catch glimpses of Alice and John looking at me.

I think all three of us don't know what to say. Mickey's dead. Today was his funeral. It's been a heavy day for all of us, except Melanie.

She's still full of smiles and facts about penguins. It melts my heart. If it wasn't for her presence, the room would be entirely silent.

John looks at me. "Michael... I mean, Mickey was a good man."

Alice glances at her husband, then at me, and down to her plate where she starts cutting into her steak. John shakes his head and makes a clicking sound at the side of his mouth.

"That boy could drive me crazy," he lets out a laugh. "But he was, overall, a good person. A good stepson. No matter what troubles he was in near the end, I try to remember the good times." He raises his glass. "To Mickey."

Alice looks at me.

I raise my glass and join his gesture, and Alice follows. Melanie smiles and raises her glass of water, spilling some on the table. Alice quickly wipes it up with a napkin.

John clears his throat again. "Hopefully he's found some peace now. In a better place."

The three of us drink from our wine glasses as

Melanie watches us. Her mouth is wide and eyes full of expression. "Mickey," she says. Her eyes fix on mine. "Mickey. Back." She smiles. "Sleeping," she says in a silly tone.

I lower my head and cover my eyes. Alice had said she was struggling today.

No, Mickey won't be back. He'll never be back.

But how do you tell a young girl with a disability that?

When I lower my hand from my face, Melanie is still looking at me. "Mickey. Back," she says again.

Alice pats her daughter's hands. "We talked about this, Melanie."

"Mickey back!" Melanie says again, raising her voice with a sense of urgency.

John takes a deep breath. Alice tries her best to calm her daughter.

"It's okay, Melanie," Alice says. She smiles. "Here, help me with the dishes and I'll read you that book about Antarctica."

Melanie looks at me, and back at her mother. "Antarctica?" she says with a wide smile. "Penguins!" Her voice is so enthusiastic that it puts a smile on both John and me.

Alice gathers a few dishes from the table and Melanie picks up her own. The two of them go to the kitchen together.

"Sorry," John says to me when we're alone. "This will be hard for Melanie. We keep trying to explain it but it's not getting through."

I shake my head. "No, it's fine. Really. Thanks again for letting me stay here with you guys."

John nods. "Of course," he says. "Any time you want

to come by town for a visit, you're always welcome here."

"I was wondering if you had the card for the detective on Mickey's case," I ask.

John nods. "It's in the kitchen somewhere. I can get it for you."

As he stands up from the table, Melanie takes small steps towards me. Her head is down with a large frown on her face. When she is near me, she reaches out for my hands, her head still lowered.

I grab them. "Is everything okay, Melanie?"

"Sorry," she says in a hushed voice. Alice walks up behind her and rubs Melanie's back.

"She's worried she upset you, about Mickey," Alice says.

"Oh," I say. I grip Melanie's hand and smile. "I'm okay, sweetheart."

"Sorry, sister," Melanie says with a somber tone.

Alice lets out a heavy breath. "Melanie, we talked about this," she says with a harsh tone. "Sarah isn't your sister. Mickey wasn't your brother."

"It's okay," I say to Alice. "I don't mind her calling me that if she likes. Since staying here she's already called me sister a few times. I think I even encouraged it." I lower my head until I can see Melanie's eyes. "You can call me sister if you like."

John comes up to me, a card in his hand. "Here's the officer's card." I immediately let go of Melanie's hands and grab it.

CHAPTER 8

Brother

As my sister's on the phone with the detective, I watch Melanie in her craft room. She sits quietly at her table, making another drawing. Her *artwork* she called it.

I have a pile of them at my house.

She's already made a few pages since sitting at her station. She's creating a stack of artwork beside her. The one on top has a stick figure with a large circular belly and a beak where its nose should be. I already know what it is.

A penguin, of course.

The penguin has a smile under its beak for some reason and appears to be dancing with its stick feet and hands all over the place.

I smile, thinking about her love for the creatures. What is it about penguins that Melanie loves so much?

I'm not entirely sure. They are cool animals, especially to watch in person. I wanted to bring her to the Calgary Zoo one day but Alice wouldn't allow it.

I can't exactly blame her, especially now that I can reflect on what I was like.

Alice was one step away from asking me to take a drug test every time I entered her house. I take in a deep breath, understanding her reservations about me.

With the clear mind I have after my death, I'm not sure I'd let someone like me through the front door or be alone with their child either.

I was a good person, I remind myself. I would never be high around Melanie. As I think about the words, I know that's not exactly true.

I've knocked on my stepfather's door drunk and high before. Alice had every right to be upset with me. She made sure that I understood the boundaries.

Do not be high and talk to her daughter.

Alice is cleaning dishes in the kitchen. I look over at her and my smile from Melanie's love of penguins disappears.

She had every right to be upset with me.

I wasn't even John's real son, and yet I was baggage from his previous marriage. John put up with me, even though he didn't have to. He helped me when I needed it. And despite that, I treated them like garbage.

Melanie would sometimes call me *brother*. It warmed my heart when she did. I'm sure she doesn't know how much impact her presence in my life made. She was the one pure thing who never looked at me the way others had.

The way my stepfather had. The way Sarah would. I can only imagine what my mother would have thought of me had she seen how I was the years after her life ended.

Sarah continues to chat with the detective on the phone. I wonder what the two are saying to each other. The last thing I want to do is hear it, though. I know it's about me. About my murder.

Sarah is too stubborn to leave town with what happened to me unsolved.

She's always been stubborn. Sarah is the definition of

the term 'Never Give Up.'

When we were eleven and one summer her bike was stolen from our backyard, she was determined to find it. Mom said she'd buy her another one, but Sarah refused. It was now her mission to find her yellow bike with the white basket on the front.

First, she made a hand-drawn map of the streets near us. She systematically went down the nearest neighborhood first, crossing off areas with a line when she felt satisfied she'd looked thoroughly enough. Sometimes I'd help her but would remind her each time that what she was attempting was useless.

For a whole week, my eleven-year-old sister was determined to find it, and eventually, she did. It was in the backyard of a house several streets away. We didn't know what kid lived there.

Sarah knew it was her yellow bike, not only because of the white basket, but a scratch on the side that her bike had from when she had a wicked fall that summer.

She immediately told Mom about it, and she called the police. But the officers explained they had no recourse to get the bike back for Sarah. The current owners denied stealing it.

Brother to the rescue.

One night, I snuck into that backyard and rode it home. I don't think I've ever made my sister as happy as I had that day.

That was Sarah, though. She would have extended her search to the whole town if she had to. I smile, thinking how different I am from her.

I take a seat on the empty chair beside Melanie. "What are you making now, little sister?" I peer over her shoulder to see for myself.

She's drawn three stick figures floating around inside what appears to be a car. For a change, none of the characters are penguins. The one in the front seat is undoubtedly Alice. In the backseat of the car is a smaller stick figure with long hair. It's Melanie, of course.

Slightly behind her in the car is a stick figure I've seen many times. She always gives me spiky hair like Bart Simpson for some reason. I smile, taking in her picture, as she takes a black crayon and colors the outside of the car.

As with most of her stick figure creations lately that involve people, no one is smiling. Unless it's a penguin, every person in her drawings has a stoic face.

My sister thanks the officer she's talking to and slides her phone into her jeans pocket. She turns to John. "Any way I could have your car for a bit?"

John raises his eyebrows. "Uh, well I was about to leave for the store." He looks over at Alice and shouts at her, "Are you okay with Sarah taking your van? Or wait, doesn't Melanie have swimming or whatever?"

Alice doesn't turn and continues washing a dish. "No, John, swimming is Thursdays." She turns to Sarah. "Keys are in the key drawer," she says, nodding towards a drawer near her. "I'd grab them for you but my hands are all greasy."

"Right," John says. "Swimming is on Thursdays. I can't keep up with the kid's schedule."

I walk into the kitchen and open a drawer.

"Wrong one," Alice says. "It's the next one over."

"Thanks Alice," Sarah says, grabbing a keychain full of keys. "This one, right?" Alice nods. Sarah thanks Alice again before heading towards the front door.

I stand up from the table as Melanie viciously blackens the page with her crayon. "Okay, little sister," I say. "Gotta go. See you again soon. Keep making drawings, hun. Maybe happier ones."

She smiles to herself, and for a moment, I wonder if she somehow heard me. "Mickey. Back," she whispers.

My face drops. I won't be back. I'll never be back. And yet, she'll continue to think otherwise no matter what Alice or my stepfather tell her. I shake my head in disbelief. If I had a heart in my current form, it would be broken at the idea.

I don't say another word before I join my sister. "Where are we going now, sis?"

I enter the car with her, and it doesn't take long for me to figure out our destination as Sarah speeds through town. Soon enough, we're outside my house.

For some reason, I expect police tape to be around the whole building, but it looks like how it had before I died. As if nothing terrible happened inside.

She looks at the front door and lowers her head. I can only imagine what she's thinking right now. The house was still technically hers after Mom's death. Now that I'm gone, it's all hers.

I'm sure if I was her, my first thought would be selling the house as quickly as possible. Our mother rotted away from cancer until she died in her bedroom. Then... I died as well. And it all happened in this house.

Why keep a house like this in your life? All it would do is cause pain.

"Sis," I tell her as she ignores me. "Just leave. Go back to Toronto. Back to university. Get far away from Pinewood Springs. There's no reason to stay. Don't stay for me." She doesn't answer me but coincidentally puts the car in drive and starts to slowly move down the street.

I don't understand why I'm still here. What's the

point? Why torment myself like this? I'm dead. I was killed. Following my sister in her stages of grief won't make things easier for me.

I need to accept my reality, that I'm no longer alive.

The dark sky lightens a moment. I stare at a streak of light that goes across the night sky.

I turn to my sister. "Let's just go back to John's house. Let's hang out with Melanie. Make penguin pictures with her. Let's just make the best of this."

Even if Sarah could hear me, somehow I know she wouldn't listen. She continues to drive down the main strip and parks outside the police station.

"What are we doing now?" I ask.

I follow Sarah as she steps out and goes inside the building. She speaks to a receptionist at the front and asks for Detective Drayson.

"Why, sis?" I say.

Soon, a tall man in plainclothes greets Sarah.

"Detective Bill Drayson," he says to her. They shake hands. "Is it okay if we talk in the back?"

Before Sarah can answer, he turns and she follows him through the office. The detective opens a door and waves for Sarah to enter.

He sits behind his desk and Sarah sits in front of him. I scoff as I take an empty chair beside her.

"I know you have questions, Ms. Roland," the detective says. "It didn't feel appropriate telling you over the phone."

"I understand," Sarah says, nodding. "Thanks for meeting with me so late."

He smiles. "I'm always here." He shuffles some paperwork on his desk and puts it in a neat pile. I catch a glimpse of a picture attached to one of the documents. It looked like a bloody head.

I cringe when I wonder if this is my file. Was that my head that was bloody?

"I understand the funeral was today. I'm truly sorry. My condolences to you... So, what would you like to know?" the detective asks.

Sarah takes a deep breath. "Well... can you tell me how you found my brother?"

He nods. "John Berthume called into our station asking for a welfare check when Michael didn't show up to work one day."

"Mickey," I say. I could never stand the name Michael.

"So, when you went to my brother's house, what did you find?" Sarah asks.

The detective clears his throat. "Only blood. Enough of it to suspect something bad had happened. We still hoped that perhaps he'd be alive, though, and considered him missing."

Sarah bit her lip and her eyes lit up. "I remember that," she says. "Your constables had the gall to tell us that he hurt himself and ran away was the initial thought."

Detective Drayson purses his lips. "The investigation could have been handled better initially, you're right. Once I got involved in the missing person's case, however, we tried our best to find him. His car was still parked outside. There was no sign of a break-in. We canvassed the neighbors."

"What about his girlfriend?" Sarah says. "Jenn, or his friends?" She shakes her head. "I can't even remember their names, I'm so flustered."

"Do you need something to drink? Coffee or water?" the detective asks.

Sarah tries her best to calm her nerves. "No, that's

okay, thank you."

The detective nods. "Ms. Jenn Harring refused to speak to me."

"What?" Sarah says.

I shake my head in disbelief. Jenn lied at my funeral today. Now she's refusing to talk to cops. I wonder why? I curse out loud, but nobody seems to mind.

"Can she do that?" Sarah asks. "Just not talk to you?"

The detective nods slowly. "Unfortunately, yes. She's not under arrest, so we can't force her to answer anything. We don't have enough evidence to arrest her."

Sarah lowers her head. "What about his two doofus-looking friends?"

The officer sorts through some paperwork on his desk. "I believe you're referring to Mr. Jake Matthews and Mr. Lenny Mercer. Well, they did agree to speak to me, separately. They both had the same story. They drank at a bar called Woods Bar and Grill all night. They never saw your brother the day he was murdered. The bartender backs up their story."

"What is happening here?" I say out loud. I stand up and attempt to slam the table, but my hand slips through the desk. "Why are my friends and girlfriend lying?" In a fit of rage, I try to toss the paperwork of my murder off the policeman's desk. As my hands slide through the file, a slight breeze lifts a page. "I saw Lenny and Jake that day!" I shout.

I turn from them and attempt to cover my head in frustration.

"Can you tell me more about... how you found him in the woods?" Sarah asks.

"I can't hear this, Sarah," I say. I pace around the room.

"A hiker found him while going off-trail with his dog," the detective says. "Your stepfather, Mr. Berthume, positively identified him."

Sarah wipes her eyes quickly. "What do we know happened to him? How was he killed?" She wipes her eyes again.

The detective lowers his head. "I understand you want to know, but some things are not worth knowing."

Sarah looks at him coldly. "I need to know, detective."

The officer nods and sorts through some paperwork on his desk. "This is from the coroner's office," he says. "Forty-one blows to his head. He died from blunt force."

"Forty-one," I say. Jenn… What did you do to me?

"Do we have any idea what he was struck with?" Sarah asks, finding her composure.

I shake my head. "This is dark. I can't listen to this." The worst part is, I can't even cover my ears to pretend to not hear it.

"We're still investigating it."

"How could someone bring a body through the woods like that?" I ask. "Could there be more then one killer?"

He nods. "That's entirely possible, but there were indications that someone placed your brother on a blanket or something like that, to bring his body through the woods. In the heat of the moment, when adrenaline is pumping, you'd be surprised what someone can do. It does appear that at some point that energy wore off. The murderer attempted to bury your brother. Some of the ground was dug up near his body, but the killer gave up."

Sarah nods and stands up. "Thanks again for speaking with me tonight." The officer gets up and the two shake hands again.

"I need to ask before you leave," the detective says, "what type of relationship did you have with your father? Your biological father, I mean."

"None," Sarah answers curtly. "We don't even know him. He moved far away from Pinewood Springs after we were born. Why?"

"We spoke to him after Michael's death. Were you aware he only lives in Calgary?"

Sarah's eyes widened. I look at my sister and purse my lips.

"I didn't know that," she says. "He only lives an hour away? Is he a suspect or something?"

The detective shakes his head. "Not really. Your father, Mr. Derrek Madson, did say that he was in contact with Michael a week before his death. Were you aware of that?"

Sarah takes a deep breath. "Mickey talked to our dad? About what?"

"To catch up, apparently," Detective Drayson answers.

As the officer says the words, I roll my eyes. That's the last thing I'd want to do with my father. I was just as surprised when I discovered he lived near me. My own dad, and he couldn't care less I was alive. Well, now I'm dead and his sentiment is the same.

"So my father knew Mickey was killed?" Sarah asks and the officer nods. "Why didn't he come to the funeral?"

I turn to the officer, waiting for a response as well. Sarah and I share the same look of disappointment. I hadn't even thought about that. Why wasn't my own dad at my funeral? His only son, and he wasn't there.

The detective clears his throat. "I'm not sure about that," he says. "From what I understand, your brother and him didn't have the best relationship."

Understatement of the century.

"Are you able to give me his address?" Sarah asks.

"I'm afraid not," he answers.

CHAPTER 9

Brother

As we get into the van, I can see the sadness in my sister's face.

I'm sure she thought seeing that detective would somehow make things easier. She only has more questions, and so do I.

Jenn didn't speak to the police after my disappearance and death. Why? She lied at my funeral. Why? What is she hiding?

I wish I could scream at my sister to tell her what I know.

Sarah turns on the ignition and looks in the rear-view mirror. "You were talking to Dad?" she says out loud.

I lower my head. It wasn't one of my finer moments. I was desperate.

"Why did you reach out to him?" Sarah says to herself. If only I could answer.

"We're wasting our time talking about him." Sarah doesn't respond. Instead, she takes in a deep breath and puts the van in drive and turns into the street.

"Sis, can you hear me?" I say. "I swear sometimes that you can. You can sense me or something. We have that twin connection. I feel like you can hear me on some level."

Sarah puts on the radio and drowns out my whispered sounds that she can't hear. I sit back in the chair, defeated. "You need to look at Jenn! She lied. You don't know that, but she did. She's hiding something. She did this to me?"

I see an image of the picture from my file on the detective's desk. My battered head. The night it happened, all I felt was a thud. It was as if I suddenly fell asleep. When I opened my eyes, I was dead.

None of this makes sense to me.

A flash of headlights illuminates the inside of the van. Sarah covers her eyes for a moment and puts down the visor in the rearview mirror. She continues to look outside as she drives down the road.

"Where are we going now, sis?" I ask. "It's getting late." The vehicle behind us continues to strike us with its high beams. I shake my head. "And who is this jerk behind us?" I always hated people who put floodlights on their vehicles.

When I turn to look, I can't make out much besides a red truck. Sarah looks in the rearview mirror again. She looks out the side mirror as well and finally turns her head.

"Stop tailgating, you dick!" I scream. If I were alive, my road rage would be in full effect by now.

Thankfully, as if the driver behind us heard me, they back off and get more distant. Sarah takes a deep breath again.

"Let's just go back to John's," I say again, but when we pass the intersection to go there, I wonder what my sister has in mind.

We pass the less populated areas and soon it's only

Sarah on the road, the truck behind us. Suddenly the truck gets closer again, its lights brightening up the entire van.

"The jerk is still behind us," I say as Sarah nods to music on the radio. It's an old song from the nineties that I remember Mom loved by Alanis Morissette. It's building up to the chorus and Sarah's getting really into it.

Now this is torture. Not only am I dead but I'm forced to watch carpool karaoke starring my sister. I smile as she continues singing. Suddenly, I can't help but join in with her. The chorus comes to an end and we both sing terribly in unison.

I laugh as Sarah continues to drive. The bright lights from the truck behind us suddenly get closer again.

"Who the hell is that behind us?" I say.

Sarah lowers the music and looks at her rearview mirror. I turn and look, and this time I can make out people inside. I finally recognize the vehicle and who it belongs to.

"Jake?" I whisper. I make out a second person in the truck. "Lenny? What are you two doing?"

Sarah takes a deep breath. She turns suddenly down a road and Jake follows us. It's becoming obvious that they're following us.

"What the hell are you two doing?" I say again.

"What do I do?" Sarah says to herself, realizing the danger she's in. I don't think she realizes who they are though. I do, which is why I'm more afraid for her.

If only she could hear me.

"Just drive back home!" I shout to my sister.

Sarah looks back at the truck in the rearview mirror. She suddenly pulls off the road to the side and puts her foot on the brake.

"What are you doing?" I say to her. "Don't stop! Hightail it out of here. You don't know these people, sis. I do. They're messed up. Don't stop. Go home. Back to John's house."

The red truck slowly drives past us. I see Lenny peering into the van. Sarah does her best not to look at them.

The truck pulls off the road ahead of us and comes to a complete stop. Their brake lights turn the entire van red now.

If I had a breath to hold, this is where I'd remember to breathe. I'm just as panicked as Sarah is.

"Let's just reverse and head back to the police station," I say. "Come on, let's go."

Instead, Sarah continues to look out the window at the truck.

After a moment, the truck turns back onto the highway. I'm in sheer terror, just as I imagine Sarah is, until I realize they're not turning around. Instead, they continue driving down the dark road.

Sarah takes a moment to collect herself and reverses back down the road.

"What were they doing?" I say out loud. "My friends were following you, Sarah. Why?"

Sarah stops at the intersection she turned at, but instead of heading towards John's house, she goes back to the road she started on.

I'm at a loss for words sometimes when it comes to my sister. Had this been any other person, they'd just go home, but of course, not Sarah. She has a destination in mind, and two of my manic friends in their truck won't deter her.

She turns down a dark road and follows a large,

fenced property. It finally hits me where we are. We were here hours ago.

"You're going back to the cemetery, sis? It's going to be closed. It's too late. Let's just go back to John's."

Sarah doesn't listen and instead creeps up to the front gate. When she realizes the gate is closed, I smile.

"Told you, sis. Closed. Let's just go. It's been an emotional day for us both."

Instead of reversing, she turns off the van and exits. I shake my head in disbelief. "You are the most stubborn person I know, sis. It's closed."

I watch her examine the gate and try to open it. When she can't, she looks at the gaps in the fence and easily slips through it.

I scoff and roll my eyes. "What are you doing now?"

CHAPTER 10

Sister

A cold shiver runs up my back and I wonder if I should just leave and go back to John's house. After that weird incident on the road with the truck driver, I was worried something was happening. The truck driver must have been lost or something.

I thought for sure they were following me, but then they took off.

Being in a cemetery at night is just as creepy as it sounds.

After speaking with Detective Drayson, I felt the urge to come back to visit my brother. I felt sick the entire time I listened to what my brother's murderer did.

Forty-one blows.

Who could do that to Mickey? Why would they do that to Mickey?

Detective Drayson's still looking at this as a potential robbery. It just doesn't make sense. Things around the house were tossed around though. Cushions were moved. The couch was at an angle. The fridge and freezer were left open.

Perhaps the person who killed Mickey was just a criminal, looking to get a free high at the expense of my brother's life.

I think of his girlfriend, Jenn. What if she was involved?

My stomach is in knots as I continue down the paved walkway. I had let my thoughts run wild and now I'm completely disoriented as to where I am.

Just leave, a voice inside me says. What are you doing here?

I know why I'm here. Someone murdered my brother and I seem to be the only one who cares about that. Everyone, including my stepfather, talks about how Mickey went down a dark path in life. No one seems that surprised that he ended up murdered. It's as if they feel Mickey was asking for it, living the life he had.

I don't think that way. As angry as I get at how Mickey changed, I don't blame him for what some psychopath did to him.

Forty-one blows to his body. The murderer then moved him to the nearby woods. With how badly his body was damaged, I can only imagine how unrecognizable he would have been when the hiker found him.

I cringe at the idea.

With the help of the full moon, I'm able to figure out where I am and can see the area where my brother's buried.

I feel something unsettling, though, as I get closer to his gravestone. I suppose being alone in a cemetery would make anyone feel that way.

Only I'm not alone.

I stop when I see a silhouette of a tall man standing at my brother's grave. He's looking down at the tombstone.

My eyes widen and now my stomach is in knots.

The killer? Could this be him? I've heard stories about how evil people go to the graves of the people they hurt.

With the limited light from the night sky, I make out what he's wearing, which has me even more freaked out. The tall man is wearing a dark suit and a white button up shirt. Suddenly, his head begins to turn towards me.

I snap out of being a deer in headlights and hide behind a small tombstone, praying the stranger didn't see me. My heart is beating so hard I'm worried it will burst through my chest.

I peek over the tombstone and still see him, only he's looking directly at me now. He turns his full body towards me, and I quickly duck back down.

What should I do? As if the answer wasn't obvious enough, I hear a voice in me that screams, "Run!"

I jet as fast as I can towards the front gate. I feel eyes on me as I try to escape. When I turn back to see if the man in the suit is close to me, I panic even more.

He's no longer there.

It's as if he was a ghost. A figment of my imagination. The type of story people share at campfires.

For a moment, I think about going back and finding the man. He's the killer. He was the one who hurt my brother and dragged his body into the woods.

He's not a ghost. He's real.

I consider calling the police, but I'm not even sure what I'd say.

Before I can make a decision on what to do, I hear movement in the bushes in front of me. I stop running and watch in horror as the tall man comes out of the darkness.

He brushes off some leaves from his jacket and smiles at me. It takes a moment for my brain to register the horror of what I'm seeing until I realize it's not a nightmare.

"Sarah?" the man says to me. His grin widens.

CHAPTER 11

Sister

"Drew?" I say, amazed that my ex-boyfriend from high school is standing in front of my brother's tombstone in the middle of the night in a suit.

"You scared me half to death." He laughs.

"You! I was terrified when I saw you in the dark." I look around the dark cemetery. "What are you even doing here?"

"I have a better right to ask that question, Sarah," he says with a thin smile. "I thought you were like a graverobber or something." Suddenly his grin vanishes as he looks back towards Mickey's gravestone. "Of course, you don't need to answer that question. I'm sorry. I know this must be hard."

I lower my head. "It is. I guess I just wanted to visit him. Feels weird to say." I look at Drew, confused. "You know he had a funeral during the daytime, right?" I ask.

Drew nods. "Of course."

I scoff. "Well, do you always hang out in cemeteries at nighttime... in suits?"

He gives a wry smile. "Sort of, yeah. It's kind of my job now."

"Job?"

He points to a dimly lit building on the other side of the graveyard. "I work here."

I let out a laugh, waiting for him to say the punchline, but when he doesn't, I can't help but clarify. "You actually work here?"

He nods. "I'm a mortician now." He lowers his head and lets out a laugh. "I know, I know. I didn't expect to have this type of career either."

I shake my head in disbelief. "You actually work here?" I say, still dumbfounded at the idea that my ex-boyfriend, in some bizarro world, would end up working with dead people. "I just never thought you were interested in a job like this?"

He nods. "It started off as a summer job, helping around the grounds after high school ended. Somehow, I worked my way up to mortician."

"Why didn't you come to the funeral during the day?"

He takes a deep breath. "It's weird, I guess. I work with many people who pass away in Pinewood Springs. This place isn't too huge. Many times, I end up working with people I know. People who I've seen in town at the local Walmart or whatever. I was truly surprised when Mickey was brought in."

I imagine the work Mickey needed after knowing what happened in the final moments of his life. Part of me wants to ask, but I know it's too morbid and I'd rather not know.

What exactly did my ex-boyfriend do with his body? I can't imagine. Drew would have had his work cut out for him with Mickey. It was a closed-casket funeral though. There was no way to have an open one with the damage.

"I'm sorry," Drew says again.

"So, you didn't want to come to the funeral because it was Mickey?" I ask.

He shrugs. "I guess I was nervous about seeing you again. I don't know. Things weren't great before you left."

Understatement of the century. He broke my heart into itty bitty pieces and stepped all over the mess. Seems only right that we meet again at a cemetery, now that I think of it.

"I just wanted to pay my respects to him, I guess," Drew says. "It's easier to do when nobody is around." He looks back at the tombstone. "Have you spoken to the police about your brother's case?" He purses his lips. "I can only imagine what you're going through. Not knowing why or who did this must be the worse."

"It is," I confirm. I ignore his questions about the investigation. I'm not sure if I'm even supposed to share much of what Detective Drayson told me. "The police will find out who did this soon."

He looks surprised. "Good. I hope so." He looks around the graveyard and smiles. "Well, I guess you came here for a reason, and it wasn't to talk to the mortician. Listen, of course you're not supposed to be here right now, but you get graveyard hall pass tonight since you know important people around here."

I smile. "Thanks, Drew," I say. "Really. I'm happy to run into you again. If it happens again, please let it not be at night in a graveyard though."

He laughs. "Are you in town for a while?"

"Maybe," I say. "I'm not sure when I'm leaving yet. I'm staying with my stepfather and his wife."

"Alice," Drew says. "I've seen her and her daughter a lot around town… Well, I want to say have a good night, but that doesn't seem right. I guess I'll see you again sometime, and not at my work... after hours." The smile from his face vanishes quickly. "And, again, I'm sorry."

I thank him again and we awkwardly stare at each other for a moment. It's like both of us are not sure how to leave the conversation. Should I wave? A quick hug? I look at his soft lips and wonder what it would be like to kiss them again.

He was always a good kisser. I loved our make out sessions when we were younger. I thought I'd tire of his lips, but we could kiss for hours and not realize it.

"Bye," he says. He takes a step towards me and for a moment I think Drew's made the decision for me. Only he walks past me.

I watch him as he goes back to the building near the rear of the cemetery. I'm not sure what morticians tend to look like. I don't think I've ever met one. Something tells me, though, that my ex-boyfriend must be the most handsome mortician that's living.

I collect my thoughts and remind myself why I came here. I look towards my brother's tombstone. I feel less nervous walking around the graveyard at night knowing Drew's around. I don't see any more scary figures in the dark either. All I see is my brother's grave.

I notice a small bouquet of flowers there. They weren't from anyone at the funeral. I know that for sure. Below the flowers is a note that nearly flies away with the breeze. I quickly step on it and grab it before it does.

I lift up the note to read it. Even in the dead of night, I manage to read the words clearly, and a shiver runs down my spine. I read the handwritten words again to make sure I'm not seeing things.

"I'm sorry."

CHAPTER 12

Brother

My sister drives frantically back to the police station, the letter firmly in her hand the whole way. When she enters the building, she again talks to the front desk clerk and asks to speak with Detective Drayson.

Thankfully for Sarah, he was still at the office. This detective seems to live at the station. How has my murder not been solved already with him on the case?

Detective Drayson comes to the front to greet us, well, mostly Sarah. Again, he waves us to the back and asks Sarah to go over what she found.

She tells the officer how after running into her ex-boyfriend, now a mortician at the cemetery, she found the note on the grave. He asks to see the note and she hands it to him.

"This has to mean something, right?" she says anxiously. "I mean, why would they be sorry?"

The detective grimaces and takes out an evidence bag from a drawer in his desk. "This may mean nothing at all, Ms. Roland. You said your brother had contentious relationships with many people."

"I wouldn't put it that way," I interject to no one's attention.

"That's right," Sarah says.

"Well," the detective says, "this could be someone's version of coming to terms with his death. Sorry about how things went. This could mean many things. It's easy to jump to anything you see being a clue. It's normal to be hypervigilant, but I don't think you should have high hopes here."

"I understand," Sarah says.

"You were the only person who touched it?" he asks. Sarah nods. "What about this other person you saw? Mr. Picktin? Did he touch it?"

"Not that I know of," Sarah says.

"Did you see if it was him who put it there?" the detective asks.

She shakes her head. "It was too dark. I should have asked him but instead I came right back here hoping to find you."

'Well," the detective says, making clicking noise with his mouth, "we should probably collect your fingerprints." He picks up the bag and examines it. "Do you recognize the handwriting?"

I stand behind the detective, looking over his shoulder. "Nope."

"No, I don't," Sarah says as well. She shakes her head. "I think this means something. It has to. There must be cameras at the cemetery grounds. What if we get the footage and check to see if anyone else came to the grave with flowers in their hands?" Sarah scoffs. "I should have talked to Drew."

The detective stands up from his desk. "I know you have a lot vested in the outcome of this investigation, but it's best you let the police handle this. There are proper ways to do things. I'll look into this, and if you think of anything else, call me."

I scoff. "You are telling my sister what to do?" I say with a single laugh. "Good luck, copper. You may as well arrest her if you want her to stop."

"When are you going to follow up on this?" Sarah asks. "Tonight?"

"See what I mean, detective?" I say with a smirk. "That's Sarah."

The detective stands up from his desk. "On my way home, I'll drive by the cemetery and try to reach the mortician."

"Drew," Sarah confirms.

The detective nods. "Did Drew and your brother know each other?"

"Not really. They only knew each other through me."

"Well, it's still worth looking into," the detective says. "Please contact me with any other updates or questions, but…" He looks at his watch. "I'm about to leave, and I'll be away tomorrow for this conference I have in Calgary. I should be back the day after."

"So you won't be looking into this letter?" Sarah says again.

Detective takes a deep breath. "I know this is hard, and this is a mandatory conference that I have to attend, but I promise you, I'm putting in my time on your brother's death."

"Murder," Sarah corrects him. She looks away. "Sorry, today has been an emotional day." She looks outside into the parking lot. "I think there may have been someone following me today, when I went to the cemetery." Sarah tells the detective about the red truck.

"Did you see who it was?" Detective Drayson asks.

"I did," I say, raising my hand, not that the officer will

choose me to speak. "Jake Matthews and Lenny Mercer! My supposed friends were tailing my sister... My ex-girlfriend was lying about being with me the day I died. I have all the answers for you, detective. If only you could hear me!"

"Maybe they were not following me," Sarah says, confused. "I was just freaked out."

The detective nods. "It's natural to be scared. Someone killed your brother. That person is still free. It's easy to get paranoid, especially around the people who knew Mickey. Right now, you're hypervigilant. Everything could be something ominous. The letter you found, the person you felt was following you. Likely it's nothing."

Sarah nods. "So, when will I hear back from you about the letter and any new information?"

I laugh again. I can't help it. This poor detective will find out the hard way how much of a stickler my sister will be until my killer is found. The poor guy doesn't appear to have a life outside of the police station already.

"When I can," he answers curtly. He opens his office door.

"Sorry, Detective, one last question for you," Sarah says. "When can I go back to my family home?"

The detective nods. "Forensics have processed what they needed and released the crime scene. You can move back in if you want, and from what I understand, it's now your home. But, and please take this into consideration, the evidence of what happened to your brother is still there. I'm not sure you want to see what happened."

"Nobody cleaned up the blood?" Sarah says, confused.

The detective purses his lips and nods again.

"Authorities actually don't handle the cleanup. You'll have to hire someone to do this, or do it yourself." He takes a deep breath. "My opinion, it's not worth cleaning it yourself. The cleaners can be expensive but it's worth it. Most times your home insurance will cover it. Do you know what your coverage is like?"

Sarah shakes her head in disbelief. "I have no clue. I'm not even sure if Mickey had insurance."

Detective Drayson tightens his bottom lip. "Don't traumatize yourself by doing it yourself. In fact, I wouldn't even go inside that house until it's cleaned. Do yourself a favor."

"Okay," Sarah says, slowly agreeing with the officer.

The detective goes back to his desk and takes out a business card. "I tend to recommend these guys for cleaning. They're reasonably priced and thorough." He hands the card to Sarah. She thanks him again. "No problem, Ms. Roland. Now, I'll be following up with the mortician and heading home soon. If you need something, you have my cell. Please text. I'll be in contact with you when I return from the conference."

Sarah thanks him again and leaves the office. Before I go, I wave at the officer. "Thanks." I quickly catch up with Sarah as we head out the front door.

"Was it his handwriting?" Sarah says to herself.

"Who?" I ask. "You mean Drew's? I didn't see him drop a note when you freaked out and ran away from him."

"I need to know," Sarah says.

I sigh. "Well, even if it's not his handwriting, your ex-boyfriend creeps me out."

CHAPTER 13

Sister

I sit on the bed of my stepfather's guest room, covering my face.

Today has been a lot. I'm emotionally exhausted. It wasn't enough to bury my brother today; I had to run into my ex-boyfriend and find a mysterious note on Mickey's gravestone.

"Sorry."

That's all it said. What could it mean? The detective feels it could be nothing, although he's still willing to look into it. I look at the clock on the nightstand. It's nearly eleven at night.

Has the detective spoken to Drew about the note I found? How would Drew answer?

Was he the one who placed it there?

I have so many thoughts running through my mind that I'm too exhausted to lay my head on the pillow. I feel like I need to stay awake. I wonder if Detective Drayson will call. I think about texting him.

I need answers.

Who did this to my brother?

I think of the conversation I had with Detective Drayson. He was right. I shouldn't have asked for details on what happened to Mickey. All I can think about is what the murderer did to my brother. My imagination runs wild with images of him being brutally killed in our family home.

The home that I can return to if I want to.

If I had the power, I'd snap my fingers and sell the house without even stepping inside it again. I likely wouldn't have to. I'm sure John would help me in arranging for the cleaners, maybe even helping me with the bill short term until I can sell the house and repay him. Maybe I'm wrong, and I have insurance coverage for this.

I'm not overly worried. Money. I suppose I'll be getting a lot of it now once the house is sold. It's likely worth two or three times the amount Mom paid for it back when we were kids. Somehow she managed to afford a house despite being a single mother with two children.

When she passed and Mickey and I inherited it, Mickey initially wanted to sell. He wanted the cash, he said. He was already on a dark path at that time, and I knew if I agreed and sold the house, he would have sniffed or smoked it all away. Mickey would have had an even earlier death than he had.

Instead, he agreed that we wouldn't sell but wanted me to let him live there essentially rent free.

I should have said no. I should have realized what Mickey was going to do with the house. I'm sure he and his junkie friends made it a point to get high there. When I did visit Pinewood Springs, which wasn't often except Christmas, I stayed at John's house. I didn't even want to go back to my family home when I saw how bad Mickey was doing.

I didn't want to see what Mickey had done to our

family home. It would be too upsetting.

Now, I'll inherit it all. A few hundred thousands worth. I'd give it all back if it meant my brother was still breathing. Not the addict he became, but the Mickey I loved.

The bedroom door creaks open. I wait a moment for someone to come through the door, but no one does.

"Hello?" I call out. No one answers. "Is someone there?"

I hear thuds running down the hallway followed by laughter from John. Melanie screams as she yells for him to stop chasing her even though it's evident that she likes it.

"No!" John yells back. "You know the rule. Brush your teeth and I will."

"Okay, Dad!" Melanie says with a silly tone. John's not her father. He's not even my father, but you wouldn't know with how they talk to each other.

I smile, thinking about them. A knock on the door brings my attention back. "Can I come in?" Alice asks.

"Yeah, sure," I say. "Of course."

Alice enters the room with a thin smile. "We haven't had much of a chance to talk today. I just wanted to see how you're doing."

I take in a deep breath. "As best I can, I suppose."

She nods. "Well, if you need to talk, I'm always around."

The conversation seems like it will be a short one as she turns to leave.

"Actually, I do have a question," I say. "How was Mickey, really? I know some stories from John, but always wondered what others thought. Was it really as bad as he made it sound?"

Alice peers outside the hallway towards the bathroom where I can hear the sink running. John's talking in a hushed voice while Melanie is bursting out laughing.

Alice turns to me and steps inside the room, closing the door partway. "I'm not sure how much you knew, and I'm sure today of all days isn't the best time to talk about this, but... Mickey wasn't well. I'm sure whatever John told you was much nicer than what was actually happening."

"Do you know much about his girlfriend, Jenn Harring, or some of his friends? Did you know them well?"

Alice shakes her head. "No. I tried my best to stay out of – sorry, I don't know how to say this without being rude – Mickey's life. I didn't really like it when he was around." She lets out an audible sigh. "I wish it was different." She looks at me quickly with soft eyes. "Sorry, Mickey put John through a lot, and my husband's a kind man. He just wanted to help."

"I understand."

She sighs again. "Please don't think I'm saying anything about you as well. I know you're not really John's daughter, and Mickey wasn't his son, but he talks about you guys like you were his kids. Just because I was tense around Mickey, don't take that to mean anything about you... I was just worried about your brother being around Melanie."

"I get it," I say, but Alice covers her face.

"John tells me how different he was before the drugs. I never knew him then, though. All I saw was how he asked for work with John's hardware store, then he wouldn't show up. How he'd promise something only to turn around and break it. Mickey would always ask John for help."

When she says that, I catch my breath. I remember listening to Mickey's last voice message he left me before he was killed. He asked for help as well.

"What did he ask John for help with?" I ask.

Alice takes a deep breath. "It would usually be for money."

I lower my head. "I see."

Alice shakes her head. "One time it was for money for rehab. We found out later he didn't use the money as intended... well, not much of it. He checked into the center and left a day after. He wouldn't tell John what he spent the rest on, but it was obvious." Alice looks at me again, tears welling up in her eyes. "I'm so sorry. Look what I'm doing. On the day of his funeral, I'm still so upset with him."

"I was angry at him too," I say, "Still am."

She wipes her eyes and nods. "Yeah, well, none of that matters now. John told me some very nice stories about how Mickey was when he was younger. You too. Sounds like before his addiction, he was a good young man. I'll try and remember him that way."

I think of what Alice said. Mickey took money from my stepfather. How many times had he done so?

"Did my brother owe John a lot of money?" I ask.

Alice takes a deep breath. "Well, I don't know the exact amount from all the times John gave him some. Sometimes John would tell him it was a loan and other times it would be to help out." She lets out a laugh. "Those two really did act like father and son," she says. "John would always try and get Mickey to see what he was doing, but they'd always end up fighting and not talking to each other for a while until Mickey needed money again and John would give him work at the store."

"It! Is! Bedtime!" John shouts in a singsong way, stomping his feet as he heads down the hallway. Melanie repeats his words and stomps to the beat as they slowly get closer to her bedroom.

Alice laughs, wiping tears from her eyes again. "He's such a good man." She turns to me. "I fell in love with him after watching how he treated my Melanie." She lets out a laugh as she listens to her daughter and husband sing their bedtime song.

I nod. "He was the best father figure I could have asked for, too." I lower my head and get upset as I say the words. Not because it isn't true but because of the thoughts running through my mind.

"You're welcome to stay as long as you need to, Sarah, okay?" I nod. "Do you know when you want to leave? You still have school, right?"

I give a thin smile. "I may just take the semester off… but don't worry. I can go back to my family house."

Alice makes a face. "No, that's okay. Stay as long as you need to," she says again.

I thank her and she quietly leaves the room before joining in on the bedtime song and dance happening in the hallway. Soon enough all three poorly attempt to sing in unison. "It! Is! Bedtime!"

I manage to lay my head on the pillow, but that doesn't stop my mind from racing even faster after my conversation with Alice. Mickey owed my stepfather money.

Why didn't John tell me?

CHAPTER 14

Sister

It's a difficult night, but I somehow manage to eventually find some sleep. When I wake, I hear John talking to Alice in the hallway, and Melanie yelling for her mother to listen to her.

"One moment, Melanie," Alice tells her. "I'm talking to Dad."

"Mom!" Melanie shouts, not caring for the response.

Part of me hopes to hear another John, Alice and Melanie song about it being morning time. Instead, the house is bustling for a normal weekday morning.

John is first to leave to go to his hardware store. Before he does, he gave me an extra key to his house. Soon after, Alice and Melanie scuttle out the door for Melanie's school. Alice asks if I need a ride somewhere. I thank her but decline.

I'm not sure where I want to go exactly but feel the need to walk around town. Reminisce a little.

What am I going to do now? Why am I still here? I think of leaving at times. I can't stop thinking about my brother's murder and my mother's death. I know I'm grieving, but my emotions are all over the map.

My eyes well up as I think about what holidays will

look like now. My brother and mother are gone. Part of me knows that John will invite me over for Christmas. He's just that type of guy. I was never his actual daughter, but he did a good job making me forget at times.

Better than my actual father.

I still can't believe Mickey was in contact with him. How often had he and our father talked? Did they visit each other? My real dad, Derrek Madson, lived an hour away from me. How long has he been living there? Did Mom know? She had told us he moved across the country after he left her alone with us.

I've only seen a few pictures of him from the 90s when he first started dating my mom. I don't even remember being around him. The only way I'd recognize him is from old pictures.

I leave John's house and walk aimlessly down the block. Pinewood Springs is not very large. Within two hours, I likely could hike my way to the town limit.

As I walk, I think about where I'll end up. When I pass the downtown area I think about going around the main strip to take in the memories. It's only been a few years that I've been away at university in Toronto, but I wonder if much has changed. Is the Old Town Arcade still down the block? When we were kids, Mickey and I would take our bikes and go there every Saturday morning. We'd be the first to step in when the doors opened.

As soon as we were inside, we'd go directly to this game called *Time Cop*. It was a shooting game. Mickey and I were always the top scorers on the game's board. We took pride in that. That entire summer the Roland twins dominated *Time Cop*. Nobody else came close. We worked good as a team, taking down the bad guys.

It would be nice to see if the arcade still exists, and

even if *Time Cop* is somehow still operational. If it is, I wonder if anybody beat my high score. But for now, I'd rather go somewhere else.

As much as I told myself I wouldn't, I know exactly where I was heading the entire time.

Detective Drayson said I shouldn't go back to my family home. He advised me to get the cleaners arranged first. He was probably right, and with every step I take, I know it, but that doesn't stop me from walking towards the house I grew up in.

Where Mom raised us. Where Mickey was killed.

As I get closer to my street, I see a building that was a wonderful landmark for me growing up. Palmwood Springs Creamery.

I'm amazed to see the small ice cream-shaped store's open. You weren't able to eat inside. You could only order your dessert to go.

I wonder if they still have my favorite flavor, maple caramel with little pieces of chocolate and pecans mixed in. After the arcade, Mickey and I would come here on the way home.

Maybe on the way back to John's, I'll stop to have a scoop or two.

Something that has changed is the graffiti sprayed on the gas station behind the ice cream parlor. The kids wanting to enjoy a chilled treat on a hot day would see the large blue phallic symbol on the brick wall.

I walk slowly down my street, taking in the sights. It has been a few years since I did. Not much has changed within that timeframe. There's still the beat-up looking playground we played on. The slide rattled to the point you thought it would fall off if you used it. I'm surprised they still let children play on it. There was a dark blue house on the corner. Who paints a house dark blue? It was such an eyesore and still is.

As I spot my house, I see an elderly woman working in the neighboring garden. Barbara Withers. Widowed a few years before I left town, Barbara was always outside in her garden doing something. Today, it looks like she's planting bulbs. I remember how lovely her garden would look each summer.

I think about calling out to her as I get closer but decide not to. Why bother her? She seems happy. Seeing me will only remind her of the terrible events that happened at the house I grew up in.

I'm about to walk up the porch steps when I realize I don't have a key. John gave me a key to his house today. What's the chances that he still has a key to mine? If John doesn't have a key, I'm not sure how I'll get inside.

That could be a question for the detective next time I speak to him. Maybe I just need to call a locksmith.

Getting inside shouldn't be too difficult, hopefully. All the nostalgia of the day helps me remember the fake rock we had in the backyard with a key inside. Mom put it there after one time Mickey and I came back from the arcade, but she wasn't home and we waited over an hour for her. The key had a Calgary Flames emblem on it, despite none of us being into hockey.

It's been years since I needed to use the key in the fake rock, and hopefully, it's still there. I walk around the side of the house and enter through the small gate into the backyard. John always kept good care of the yard when he lived with us. Now, though, it's certainly not the same. The grass is tall. The trees need trimming. Weeds dominate the garden.

Something tells me it wasn't a priority for Mickey

when he was alive. I can only imagine what the inside of the house will look like.

When I walk over to the rock garden, my eyes scan around until I see a shimmer of plastic from the fake rock. I smile as I pick it up and open it, only to find that it's empty.

What did I expect?

It's been years since I've used it. Burglars and bad guys alike would likely know what plastic fake rocks look like. I'm sure it's not recommended to have them anymore. Mickey likely got rid of the key.

Or did he?

Detective Drayson said there were no signs of a break-in. Did someone find the key, or know of the key, and use it to get inside?

Was that how the murderer was able to get in my family home and kill my brother? I toss the fake rock back into the garden and stare at my house.

CHAPTER 15

Brother

I slowly walk behind my sister as she tries to find a way into our family home. She attempts the back door and front door first. When she finds the doors locked, she attempts to open some of the windows, every so often looking around the empty streets, worried someone will see her.

Of course it's her house, only hers, now that I'm deceased, but I can still see the panic in her eyes. She's not used to sneaking into places.

As I reluctantly follow her, I try my best to tell her what I know, hoping somehow she'll understand.

"I never removed the key from the fake rock!" I shout at her. I stand beside her as she tries her best to open a locked window. "The key was there, I know it! I still use the key myself."

Even if she can't hear me, I won't admit why I still used the key. In my drunk and drugged stupors, I'd somehow manage to lock myself out of my own house at times.

Sarah didn't need to know that, though.

The idea begins to dawn on me. My killer knew of the key. How else did they get inside the house unnoticed?

As I listened to the detective talk my sister, I hoped what he said was true. My murderer was someone I didn't know. An opportunistic criminal who knew I kept drugs at my house. Maybe they'd get lucky and find something else valuable. Unfortunately for me, I just so happened to be home as well.

With Sarah's recent discovery about the key not being in the fake rock, I'm coming to understand this is not the case.

I knew my killer.

Forty-one. That's how many blows my skull and body had when my body was discovered. I know I've been thinking of this number often, but it doesn't register. Who could do that to me? Who hated me that much?

Someone I knew, someone I loved or cared for, called my friend or neighbor, viciously murdered me. Even though I have no physical body, I'm furious to the point I want to scream. No one could hear me anyway.

Sarah moves around the house to another window. As she pushes the window to the living room, it moves an inch. She smiles as I sulk.

"What are you doing here, sis?" I ask. "The detective told you not to come here until after the cleaners are finished. Of course you didn't listen." I scoff. "I'm supposed to be the stupid sibling. You are outrageous."

She manages to push the window fully open and slide into the living room. As she does, I notice my neighbor, the elderly Barbara Withers, pushing some soil over a newly planted tulip. I shake my head in disbelief.

No wonder someone could break into my house without anyone knowing and kill me. A train could run off the track and slam into my house, and as long as it didn't strike hers, my neighbor would have no clue.

I turn and Sarah is already inside. I reluctantly follow her. "Wait for me, sis," I say with gritted teeth.

Once inside, my mouth drops when I see the spots of blood that trail into the kitchen. It's as if a giant snail moved across my living room, leaving a red stain behind it. There's a large puddle of dried red on the living room carpet near the television.

That's where it started, I realize. The first blow was there. I was staring at the wall, at the family picture, when someone crept up behind me and took my life away.

How fair is this?

Someone killed me and now I'm forced to see the evidence of how it happened.

Sarah looks just as shocked as me. She stands over the area of red in the living room, thinking the same thoughts I had. X marks the spot. Well, in this case, a large stain of my life's blood.

"What are we doing here, sis?" I ask again. "Why are you doing this to yourself? To me? Let's just leave."

If I were Sarah, if I still was capable of breathing and feeling my heartbeat, I'd not only leave this house but this town. What's the point of her staying? What is she doing? Trying to figure out who killed me?

"Don't bother!" I yell at her. "Leave! Leave this town. Leave me here. Just go!"

I breathe in deep, looking around the house. Home sweet home.

It's definitely not how I imagined. Besides the areas of blood on the floor and trail of red that leads to the kitchen, the house is in complete disarray. Cushions are turned over. The fridge and icebox are open.

If I could, I'd tell my sister this is not how I lived in our family home. I wasn't the cleanest bachelor, but it wasn't this bad. I'm sure she knows it, but given how terribly everyone thinks of me, I feel the urge to say it out loud to her.

I realize that at some point, Sarah will leave. Eventually, her stubbornness to be in Pinewood Springs will subside. She'll remember why she left to begin with. Go back to university. Live a life worth living.

Where will that leave me?

I look at the dried blood again and realize maybe this is where I'm meant to stay. It is my house after all. Why not stay?

I can be that conventional ghost that haunts houses. Isn't that the stereotype of what I'm supposed to do? A family will move in and I'll try my best to communicate to them by moving chairs and throwing soda cans at them. I'll talk to their daughter and become an imaginary friend, teaching her to say dirty words and watch the horror of her parents.

Maybe ghosts do these things for something to do. They're just bored.

Even as I look at my own crime scene, I find a way to lighten the tense moment. I'd share my joke with Sarah if I could, but of course, that's impossible. My emotions change again as I watch my sister stand over the spot where I was killed. I go from lighthearted to annoyed in an instant.

"Can we just leave?" I plead with her. "What can you possibly hope to find here?"

She doesn't listen, of course. Even if she could hear my words she wouldn't listen to them anyway. She has a mission on her mind, and whatever she's thinking, I'd never be able to get her to change it.

"Let's tell the detective about the key," I try

to explain. "Tell the detective my ex-girlfriend lied. Someone used the key to get into the house, sis. Tell them!"

Sarah follows the trail of blood to the kitchen as I reluctantly follow her.

CHAPTER 16

Brother

I take my time going up the steps, following my sister. I have an idea where she's going but wish she wouldn't.

She stands in front of the first bedroom and has a thin smile on her face as she enters. It's her bedroom.

I smile as she looks around.

"I didn't move a thing, sis," I tell her. "Everything is just the way you had it before you left."

I'd throw parties at the house, but nobody was allowed in my sister's room or my mother's. They were restricted. I may have been a screw-up, but those moral boundaries, I stuck to.

She walks over to her bed and picks up a beat-up grey bunny rabbit stuffed animal. I laugh.

"What did you call that horrendous thing?" I ask. "Jumper, right? I should have burnt that thing. It's about as old as we are… you are," I correct myself.

Sarah walks over to the dresser and looks at pictures she kept in a drawer. Most of them were of Drew and her. She picks up one of her and her best friend from a few years ago. Bethany Coleman. She was pretty cute back in the day and had a huge crush on me.

"Is this a bad time to tell you," I say with a smirk, "that I made out with Beth behind the ice cream store?" I laugh. "She felt terrible despite me feeling quite happy about it. I take it she never told you." When my sister doesn't answer, I take a deep breath. "I don't feel as funny when I say stupid things and no one can hear me."

Sarah puts the pictures on top of the dresser. She walks over to her closet and opens it. Inside is a small rack that's jam-packed with clothes.

"Time for a Goodwill trip, sis," I say to her.

She bends over and pulls out a shoebox. She sifts through the contents, and I laugh when I see some of her pictures she made as a kid inside. They remind me of Melanie's artwork.

"You actually kept this kind of stuff?" I say. "Only you would."

She smiles again as she takes out a high school yearbook from our senior year under a stack of papers. She opens it to our grade. I peer over her shoulder as she looks at the old pictures of our fellow classmates. She stops when she sees herself and me beside her.

I try to pat her back but my hand wafts through her. I hate what I am, I think. I can feel her pain as she sees pictures of me and her. I wish I could do something to help her feel better.

All I can do is watch. That's all I'm good for, apparently.

She puts her hand on the picture of us and takes a deep breath.

"It's going to be okay, sis," I tell her.

When I look at the yearbook page, I can't help but notice the typography underneath our names. That year, they asked all graduates what they wanted to be after graduating. Under Sarah's name she had written: "Lawyer."

I laugh. That's so like my sister. She had a goal from high school and is managing to pursue it. I feel a strong sense of pride in her for that. She should go back to university. She mentioned she might take a whole semester off to stay in Pinewood Springs longer.

"Just leave, sis," I reason with her. "You have a life outside of this town. Go back to it."

I look down at my graduation photo. The photographer snapped my picture as I was attempting to smile and look completely stupid. I remember my friends and Sarah had a good time making fun of me for my pic. Underneath my photo when I was asked what I wanted to be, I said, "Teacher."

I can't help but laugh.

How like me, I think. I had a goal in high school but couldn't manage to do much more than smoke a joint and forget about it.

Sarah turns a few pages until she stops and examines the photos. Her eyes stop scrolling when she finds him.

Drew Pickton.

I have to admit, he was handsome back in high school and is still today. Underneath Drew's photo, I read what he said he wanted to be after graduating.

I laugh the hardest as I do. "A pediatrician!" I laugh again. "He wanted to work with newly living and ended up spending all day with the dead. How did your ex manage that, sis?"

I laugh again until I remind myself Drew spent time with my body as well. I quickly want to change the subject, but of course, I can't.

Thankfully, Sarah puts the yearbook back in the box

and into the closet. She leaves her room and heads toward the next closed door in the hallway.

"Let's not," I say. She doesn't listen.

Sarah, for once, as if she's somehow heard me, stands outside the door. After several deep breaths, she opens it. She takes a step inside but no further.

Tears well up in her eyes as she scans our mother's room. The machines that helped keep our mother alive for so long are still beside her bed.

"I didn't move a thing," I say as I peer over her shoulder into the room. "I wasn't capable of changing anything."

Together we look into our mom's room and Sarah takes another deep breath. I reach for my sister's hand and attempt to grip it tightly, but can't.

"I miss her too," I say.

Now that I'm deceased, I thought somehow I'd manage to find my mom again. We could be together. Isn't that supposed to be the only positive thing about being dead? You get to be with the ones you loved?

That's just not the case for me.

Sarah takes a step back into the hallway. She closes the door and walks through me, down the hall.

I follow Sarah as she walks toward the last bedroom in the house. Mine. It was the smallest.

Mom gave us a choice when we were kids who would get what room. Sarah, knowing that Mom would take the largest, immediately called dibs on the second largest one.

I made a stink, but really I was quite happy with the smaller room. It was furthest away from the others, and I liked the idea of having more privacy. Sarah opens the door and steps into my room.

So much for my privacy now.

Sarah stands beside my dresser and opens the bottom drawer.

"What are you looking for, sis?" I ask her. She ignores me as she rummages through my possessions.

She closes the door and kneels on the floor, knocking on the floorboards.

I laugh. "You remember. Of course you do."

As she knocks on the boards near my bed, she hears a hollow sound. She smiles and uses her key to lift the board.

My secret hiding space. When we were kids, we would hide our beloved toys in it. That way, if Mom got upset and took toys away from us, she couldn't find the ones we actually liked. Mom would have lost it had she known I was destroying our property to hide things.

Of course, as an adult, I didn't hide toys anymore.

Sarah shakes her head, and her face drops as she lifts a small bag of white powder tied with an elastic band.

I look away from her, knowing what she must be thinking.

"Sorry," I tell her. I can't look at my sister's face. I know all I'll see is her disappointment. Even in death, I can't bear the thought of what she thinks of me. "I was a different person," I say. "I was trying to be a different person." I try to cover my face but physically can't. "I was probably never going to change, was I? A train wreck waiting to happen."

She reaches back in and pulls out a notebook. I sigh as she opens a few pages.

"How about a little privacy, sis?" I say.

It's not exactly a journal, but it's close to it. I actually read a self-help book months ago. At the time, I was motivated to try and change my life. I would mark down my goals and objectives. I'd note things I was grateful for.

Sarah sits on my bed and skims through a few pages. I seriously don't want to be beside her as she reads pages of what my life was like.

I sigh, knowing that will be the case, though. I turn my head, not wanting to see her face as she reads the first page. I look at my nightstand, surprised. A picture frame is turned over.

I didn't do that.

When I look back, Sarah seems to notice it as well. She lifts it up and it's empty.

"That wasn't an empty frame when I was alive," I say in disbelief. Inside was a picture of me and Jenn.

CHAPTER 17

Sister

I walk down the stairs to the ground floor, wondering what I'm doing here. What did I think I was going to find by coming to this house?

Remnants of a life I used to love? Memories of people who loved me? None of it makes me feel that good.

The pictures of Drew brought my mind to happy times. Seeing my mother's room, though, did not. She died in that room, connected to those machines.

The powder I found in Mickey's hiding place made it worse. I thought coming here, I'd find a clue to who murdered him. I suppose I found the culprit. The reason for his death was tied up in the bag.

This house is truly empty to me now. All that remains is sadness. The same goes for this town.

If anything, seeing what I left behind in Pinewood Springs solidifies for me that I don't belong here anymore.

I'm grieving, I know. My thought process hasn't been very rational as of late.

I need to come to grips with what's happened. My brother was murdered in this house. Chances are, it was a robbery gone wrong, just like Detective Drayson suggested. People from my brother's underworld, thinking they might find drugs in the house, murdered him.

Too bad they didn't search his room properly. They left the small bag of... whatever it is behind.

I want answers as to who killed my brother. I've been on a quest to get more information. Part of me knows it's my way of dealing with trauma. I'm looking for someone else to blame so I don't have to look at myself.

I left this town. I left my dying mother. I left my brother and stepfather to play caretaker in my absence.

Mickey took our mother's death harder than me. He turned to substances to distract him from his trauma, just like I'm using his death to distract from my own.

The detective has no leads as to who killed Mickey. Chances are that me staying in town won't change that.

I should leave. Go back to school. Forget about what happened in this house. Sell it... burn it. Who cares? Just leave it. Leave behind everything that happened in Pinewood Springs.

What happens if my brother's murder is never solved, though? How many true crime documentaries have I watched where family members of a deceased person talk about wanting closure?

Do I really want to be like them?

I need to come to grips with the truth. We may never find out who did this to Mickey.

If it was a random robbery, it wouldn't explain the letter I found at the grave. It wouldn't explain the missing key that used to be in the fake rock. And then there was the picture frame in my brother's bedroom that was empty.

It's strange, but since entering this house, I feel like I'm not alone. I've had gut feelings before. Sometimes I'll reflect and those feelings come true. The voice inside you tells you not to cross the street, even though the walking man on the light is glowing white and it's your turn. When you don't move, a car barrels down the road and you realize if you had crossed, you would have certainly been struck.

Well, my gut feelings are talking to me today. Strange sensations are telling me that the fake rock, the picture frame, these are not coincidences.

I just can't explain it.

How can I explain that to the detective? I already felt a little silly calling him about the letter I found. Now I'm going to call him to tell him a key I haven't used in years is missing and so is a picture from a frame in my brother's room?

Of course, there is the journal. Detective Drayson said the crime scene was processed, but I doubt they found it. It was something I would know about, and I only remembered when I was in his room.

I'll call the detective to let him know about the journal, the missing key and the missing picture. Before I do, I'll take a look at the journal myself.

When I'm on the ground floor, I walk back into the living room and lock the window I came through. No need to sneak back outside anymore. I'll leave through the back door that I can unlock from the inside. I don't have a key to get back in. John may not even have one.

Who cares though? If I'm lucky, I'll never step back inside this house.

I take a moment to look around the living room. I cover my eyes immediately when I see the red stained carpet again. Above it on the living room wall is the picture of my mother, Mickey and me.

Taking a few steps closer, I smile, enjoying the warm memory it gives me. It was taken a year before Mom died. We took it before she started her last round of chemo. She still had all her beautiful curly hair for the photo.

I try not to remember what she looked like before I left for university. Instead, I focus on how pretty Mom was in the picture. This was my favourite photo of my family as adults. It's the same photo I have in my room in Toronto.

Strangely enough, we took it in this living room, on the same white couch that's still here. The couch now looks a lot more yellow than I remember, though. The house reeks of used cigarettes as well. An aroma that is also not familiar.

While the couch may be yellow and the house smells different, everything else in the photo is the same. Mickey still had the same living room table. On it, he still had the antique candles Mom bought at a market.

I look at the picture again and the table in front of me. The only thing missing is the white lamp Mickey and I bought for Mom for Mother's Day a few years ago. It was made of cast iron that made it look older than it was and had painted on vines and flowers.

I was the one who bought it from an online store.

The lamp is the only thing missing from the photo on the wall. I'm surprised that Mickey got rid of it, especially given how much he kept.

I have to admit, I'm surprised how well maintained the house is. When I saw the backyard, I assumed the worst. Besides the mess the killer made, the house still has a lot of its old charm.

Except for the lamp.

Strange.

For a moment, I hear a noise coming from the kitchen, followed by what sounds like someone walking.

"Hello?" I call out.

The sound stops for a moment.

I put on a wry smile, thinking I'm going crazy. Knowing what happened to my brother in this house makes it eerie being back. Seeing my brother's blood on the carpet makes it harder to be rational.

Then I hear the clinking of metal again.

My eyes follow the trail of blood in the living room and look up at the front door. That's when I see it. The handle on the door is turning. The door moves an inch as someone tries to enter.

"Who's there?" I shout.

CHAPTER 18

Brother

My sister calls out to the person at the front door, but whoever it is doesn't respond. The handle does stop turning, though, and I can hear steps thudding on the front porch.

I look back at my sister, who's wide eyed in a state of panic.

"You, stay there," I plead with her. "I'll see who it is."

I step towards the front door quietly at first, worried that whoever is there will somehow hear me. I remind myself no one can. I walk up to the door and peer through the peephole, but see no one outside.

Someone could still be on the porch though, just out of sight. I look at the curtains and put my hand out to push them to the side, only for my hand to go through them.

My sister lets out a shriek. When I turn, she's starting to move towards the kitchen. I quickly follow her.

"What's wrong?" I ask. She responds by running to the back door and locking it quickly.

After a moment, the handle starts to turn quickly.

"Go away!" Sarah shouts. Sarah covers her eyes and curls into a ball on the kitchen floor.

I stand in front of her, facing the back door. "Stay away from my sister!" I demand.

As if the person at the door heard me, the handle stops moving. I run up to the door, but there's no peephole or window to look out of. I try to push past the door, hoping my body of energy is somehow able to go through it. My hand bends at the door, though, unable to penetrate it.

"Leave her alone!" I shout again.

I look back and Sarah is slowly uncovering her face and looking around.

"Don't move, sis," I tell her. It hits me. The front door. Whoever went into the backyard may be back in the front now. I can try and see through the peephole. I run into the arch that leads into the living room, only to bounce back as if I've hit a brick wall.

I fall, managing to get to my feet quickly. It's as if an imaginary force is preventing me from entering the living room.

When I try to put my foot forward, it's stuck in the air, preventing me from going further.

I try to rush into the room, but some force is keeping me from moving an inch. I can see the front door, and I know if I could only get to it, I could see who's there.

But I can't. Something is stopping me.

I look back and Sarah's in the kitchen, slowly standing up.

"Don't go outside," I plead with her. "Call the cops!"

She takes several deep breaths and walks past me, her body moving through mine.

She steps through the arch into the living room with ease. I look at her as if she has magical powers until I walk into the room myself with no issue.

"What's happening to me?" I say. I look at my hands and back at the kitchen. It hits me. The reason I couldn't enter the living room before. It has to do with Sarah.

Sarah turns and looks directly at me. "This isn't a coincidence," she says.

I look into her panicked eyes but can't help but have a thin smile on my face. "You see me?" I ask. "You can hear me?"

Sarah takes a deep breath. "Who was that?" she asks, ignoring my question.

"I was trying to find out. I—"

"Then there was the truck that followed me yesterday," she says. "Who was that?" I'm about to answer her when she looks at my feet and back at my eyes. "Get it together, Sarah," she says.

I turn and see she's talking to the large standing mirror behind me. To herself. I shake my head. Of course she can't hear or see me.

Sarah goes up to the peephole of the door and looks outside. As she does, she unlocks the door.

"Stop!" I demand. "Don't go out there."

Sarah doesn't listen and steps onto the wooden porch. I immediately run through her and look outside for myself. No one is there.

All I hear is the humming of Barbara Withers singing to herself as she plants. Sarah takes a deep breath and manages a smile.

"Hey, Ms. Withers," she says to our neighbor. When she doesn't respond, Sarah says her name louder.

Barbara smiles at her as she looks up. "Oh, hello," she says. "Good to see you, dear. I'm very sorry about what happened to your brother."

Sarah gives her a thin smile back. "Thanks, Ms.

Withers." She looks inside and back at her. "You didn't see anyone come to the house just now?"

"Come again?" she asks. "You have to come closer, dear. Speak louder."

Sarah nods, realizing what I do. The old woman didn't notice whoever was at our door.

"That's okay, Ms. Withers," Sarah says. "Have a good day." When Barbara looks at my sister strangely, Sarah repeats herself again.

CHAPTER 19

Sister

I try my best to calm my nerves, but it feels impossible. Someone was trying to get inside. Why? What were they planning on doing once they entered?

When I yelled at them to leave, not only did they not stop trying to enter the house, but they also went into the backyard to try and open the back door.

I didn't see who it was. I could hear the scratching sound of metal as someone opened the gate to the back yard. I instantly ran to the back door and locked it.

Barbara didn't see who. Not only did she not see someone, she didn't hear anyone either. She was completely oblivious.

After speaking with her, I go back inside my house and lock the door. I also ensure all the windows were locked.

I feel more than uncomfortable staying in this house after what happened, but it was all worth it.

My gut is talking to me, and it says that it's not a coincidence that the key in the fake rock is missing, or the picture in the frame. Now the lamp is missing from the living room. It's large and heavy enough to cause damage if it was used to strike someone in the back of the head.

Especially if it was used forty-one times. I cringe thinking of it.

Someone killed my brother with a blunt object that has yet to be found. I take out my cell phone and dial the detective's phone number.

I already know what he's going to say: don't have high expectations for my discoveries. It's been years since I've stepped into my family home. Mickey could have got rid of the key in the fake rock. He could have sold the lamp or gave it away. Mickey may have been planning to put a picture in the frame in his room and just forgot.

Not exactly unlike him to do that.

The detective's number doesn't even ring and goes directly to voicemail. Great.

He's at the conference, I remind myself. He told me he may be unavailable today. I leave him a message asking for him to call me.

After I hang up, I even send a text message telling him about the missing key and picture frame. I also take a photo of the family picture in the living room, zooming in on the lamp. I explained that the lamp is now not in the house and asked if he thought this could be a potential blunt object used on my brother.

As I type out my message, I feel foolish. None of my observations may be useful. At this point, I'm probably pissing off the detective.

The journal, though. That may be useful. I plan on examining that in great detail very soon.

Suddenly, I feel anxious.

I'm not going to walk home. Whoever was at my door spooked me too much to leave. I also can't stay in this house. I look down at the red stained carpet and the trail of dried blood leading to the kitchen.

No way I'll be stepping back inside this house ever again.

I peek outside the curtains. All I see is Ms. Withers still gardening.

I'm about to call John and ask if he or Alice can pick me up, but look at the family picture again. I look at the lamp. I remember when Mom opened the box and commented on how heavy it was.

If my brother's killer was planning to rob him, what would be the chances they used a lamp to murder him with? As I think about it more, I feel silly. The idea of it doesn't make sense.

I'm being hypervigilant, as Detective Drayson pointed out. Everything's a clue when you're looking for one.

I'm looking to make sense of it all. Many times, violence and murder makes no sense. It's something that can happen in the heat of a moment. It can be planned. When you find out the reasons people kill, none of it really makes sense.

I sigh as I look at the photo.

I can't get answers from Detective Drayson about what I've found today. I have never felt as strongly as I have though that I'm right.

As if a light bulb appears over my head, I think of a way to confirm if I'm right about one of my clues.

I go through my contacts but sigh when I realize I deleted his number a long time ago. A few weeks after Drew dumped me unexpectedly, I got rid his number after many attempts to speak to him.

I google the Pinewood Springs cemetery and thankfully find a number. When I dial it, a receptionist picks up and I ask to speak to Drew Picktin. She puts me on hold for a moment, and when she comes back, she lets me know she'll transfer the call.

"This is Drew," my ex-boyfriend says a moment later. It sounds like he's in his car.

"Hey, it's Sarah," I say. "Sarah Roland." I want to roll my eyes at my own stupidity. Why did I feel the need to say my full name to him?

"Sarah," he says surprised. "Uh, how's it going?"

"Well, good, but I was hoping you could give me a ride."

"A ride?" he repeats.

"Well, maybe get some coffee too."

CHAPTER 20

Brother

When Drew pulls up outside our house, Sarah smiles. She goes through the back door, locking it from the inside, but before she closes the door, she looks into the house one last time.

"Bye," she whispers.

She takes a moment to stare at the blood trail in the kitchen, and shakes her head. I can only imagine what she's thinking, since it's likely the same as my own thoughts.

What happened to me? Who did this?

I leave before she slams the door shut. Sarah walks around the side of the house and I take my own moment to say goodbye to it.

The house my mother raised Sarah and I in. The house I inherited from Mom when she passed. The house where my own life was taken.

"Bye," I whisper the same word and quickly catch up with my sister.

Drew steps out of his vehicle when he sees Sarah. He walks around his car and opens the door for her. He's wearing his black suit again. The one that he wears around dead people all day. The idea of that freaks me out until I realize I'm one of them.

"Thank you," she says with a thin smile, surprised by his actions.

"Yeah, thanks," I say, barreling through my sister, going through her and stepping into the car.

Apparently, chivalry is not dead for the dead.

As Sarah gets into the front seat, I move into the back of the car. Drew gets into the driver's seat and starts it.

"Sorry," Sarah says, "I'm sure you were busy when I called, but I was hoping we could talk."

"Always," Drew says. "I was happy when you called."

Sarah smiles again, but this time it's larger. It's as if she's turning into a pimply teenager right in front of me as she talks to a boy she likes.

In fact, I'm pretty sure she had a similar face when she brought Drew around when we were kids.

"Thanks," she says again. As she buckles her seatbelt, her foot brushes against a grey container on the floor in front of her.

Drew's face drops. "Uh, please be careful with that," he says. He gives a wry smile. "I was sort of in the middle of something when you called but you made it sound urgent."

Sarah looks at the bin and back at Drew. "Okay," she says. "I'm not sure I even want to know what's inside that."

I let out a sigh. Way to go Drew for ruining the mood with your weird job as a mortician. What could possibly be in the grey container?

I look over Sarah's shoulder at it. White tape is across the sealed edge.

I shake my head. "Sarah, you could have just called a taxi. This is too much."

"Yeah," Drew says with a funny tone. "Sorry. Maybe try not to kick it. Or— sorry, I should really move it." Drew quickly gets out of the car and runs around it, opening the door. He reaches in and carefully removes the bin from the floor, holding it like it's a landmine. He opens the rear passenger side door and places the bin on the floor beside me.

"Really, Drew!" I shout. He doesn't listen to my complaints. "Can you at least tell me what this is beside me?" I shiver. "This is disgusting."

When Drew gets back inside, he asks where Sarah would like to go. She asks to go to Hearth and Bean, a local coffee shop in town.

As he drives, there's an awkward silence between the two. At first, Sarah came off a little flirty with her ex-boyfriend but now I can't tell if she's nervous.

They don't say a word the whole way to the coffee place. Drew opens the door to Hearth and Bean for my sister, and I step in first. Instantly a warm aroma of freshly ground coffee beans hits me. I look at the savory and sweet pastries behind the glass counter. Several people take up the tables near the stone fireplace in the center of the shop.

What a terrible time to be a ghost. I can't enjoy any of it. I used to love coming here.

Sarah buys a large coffee and Drew orders a caramel-infused steamed oak milk mocha with extra whipped cream. My sister makes a confused face as she watches Drew speak with the barista. I was just as confused as to what Drew ordered, but somehow the barista understood the order without asking him to repeat what he said.

"A bit of a fancy order for a mortician," I say. "I assumed you'd take your coffee just black for some reason."

There's another awkward exchange between them as Drew offers to pay but Sarah insists that she pays for his. Eventually, they mutually agree that Sarah will pay so long as Drew gets the next bill.

Next bill?

Already I feel like I'm third-wheeling on the worst date ever. The tension is palpable with them. Former lovers now meeting years later for coffee, casually talking about one of their siblings' murder.

They sit across from each other at a table with four chairs. I take one of the empty seats, sitting between them.

"Is someone going to say something?" I ask. "Or get me an espresso? A pastry even?"

"So," Drew says, breaking the silence, "is everything okay?"

Sarah raises an eyebrow. "Well, not really, but I'm dealing with it. I really hope I didn't interrupt your day."

Drew waves her off. "No. Don't worry about it. The dead can wait." His eyes get wide for a moment. "Sorry, that was a bit insensitive. You kind of need a sense of humor to make it in my industry."

Sarah takes a sip of her coffee, meanwhile I'm laughing hard at his joke. "Good one, Drew. Good one. My sister doesn't appreciate the punchline. I'm the dead one and not offended at all. Well done, sir."

I look at my sister as she blows into her coffee and takes another sip. I can tell she wants to say something but doesn't.

"What's wrong?" Drew asks, picking up on the vibe I have.

She takes a deep breath. "Well, I'm just wondering,

did Detective Drayson talk to you last night?"

Drew takes a moment and sips from his fancy mocha, nodding. "Yes, he did. He said a note was found at your brother's grave."

Sarah takes another deep breath. "What did you tell him?"

Drew lowers his eyes a moment before answering. "Well, I told him I didn't see a note. He asked if we had any camera footage of the cemetery grounds. I told him we're having system issues right now so we're not able to save any footage. We only have live cameras. We're in between security companies at the moment."

"System issues," Sarah repeats.

"Seriously?" I say. "System issues?"

Drew nods. "We've been having problems with kids in town. Some gang is going around tagging buildings with graffiti. Maybe you noticed the large... well, you know, that some kids spray-painted beside the ice cream place."

Sarah laughs. "Couldn't miss it."

Drew smiles. "Our system wasn't very good. We're trying to upgrade with a new provider, but we're stuck in an old contract." He sighs. "It's a real pain and the owner is really upset since one of the tombstones was graffitied as well." Sarah makes a face, and mine is equally as shocked. Drew laughs. "Thankfully, the kids didn't graffiti the tombstone with another... you know."

"Kids these days," I say. Now, I'm a tasteful non-conformist, but graffiti on the deads' graves is a little too far. I wonder if I'd feel the same way if I wasn't in my current form, though.

"The detective didn't tell you?" Drew asked. "He said he was going to tell you about the camera system after we talked."

Sarah shakes her head. "He's away right now. Actually, that's why I was hoping to talk to you."

Drew raises his eyebrows. "About what?"

Sara takes out her phone from her jeans and unlocks the screen. "Being in your position, I take it that you would have seen what happened to my brother."

"What do you mean?" he asks.

I look at my sister. "What are you getting at, sis?"

She shows him the picture of the lamp from the living room she took earlier at the house and points at it. "The police don't know what was used to kill my brother. All they know is that it was a blunt object and that he was struck..."

Sarah lowers her head, unable to finish her sentence. I lean back in my chair. Seeing my sister poorly attempting to cover her tears is hard to take in.

It seems equally as hard for Drew as well. He quickly switches chairs to one closer to her and wraps an arm around her. "It's okay," he says. "I think I get it. You thought maybe I could tell you if this lamp could have been used on Mickey?"

Sarah nods and wipes her tears. "Sorry," she says. "Well, that's right. I'm not able to get a hold of the detective and I shared this with him too. I'm not sure when he'll get back. I guess... I just need answers. I need to know what happened to Mickey."

Drew purses his lips and picks up her phone, looking at the image again. "It's hard to tell from the picture. I did take some notes on how his body was brought to us. Do you have any dimensions for the lamp?"

Sarah shakes her head. "No, but I can get them."

"Okay," Drew says. "Just text me when you figure it

out. I'll see if I can help in some way. I'm sure the detective will be of much better use, but I get it. I understand why you want me to look into it. I'll try my best for you."

"Thanks, Drew," my sister says. For a moment, the two share a longer than normal exchange.

And, just like that, I feel like I'm third-wheeling again.

"I take it you don't have my number anymore," Drew says. "Since you called the cemetery number and, well, it's been a while."

Sarah fidgets in her chair and takes another sip of her coffee. "Uh, no."

Drew gives a thin smile. "I still have yours. I'll text you so you'll have mine again. Let me know when you figure out the dimensions and I'll see what I can do."

"That means a lot," she says. The two look into each other's eyes. I wonder if I looked as stupid as they do when I looked at my girlfriend's face.

"You're staying with John still?" he asks.

"That's right," she says.

Drew nods. "Okay. Good to know. He seems like a decent guy, your stepfather. I've been to his hardware store a few times and he still gives me a discount because we dated." He laughs. "I was very surprised when he picked up the bill for the funeral."

Sarah's eyes widen. "John paid for Mickey's funeral?"

Drews mouth gapes open. "Uh, well, yeah."

She leans back in her chair. "Was it a lot?"

Drew makes a face. "I'm not sure if I was supposed to say that to you… When do you go back to Toronto?" he asks, changing the subject.

Sarah takes a deep breath, and I'm still dumbfounded by my stepfather's graciousness. "Still not sure yet," Sarah answers.

The two continue to finish their drinks and the conversation becomes awkward again. When they finish, Drew offers to give Sarah a ride to John's but Sarah asks for one to a car rental business instead.

I reluctantly sit in the back of Drew's car again, the grey container staring at me. With every turn he takes or bumps in the road, I'm terrified that it will open and fling its contents at me. Even the living will be able to hear my screams if that was to happen.

Sarah and Drew are still quiet as he drives into the parking lot of the rental company.

Before Sarah leaves, she thanks Drew again.

"It was good to see you," Drew says. "I hope we can... maybe see each other again before you leave." When Sarah doesn't answer immediately, he fumbles on his words. "Well, you know, if you want."

Sarah smiles wide at him, and for a moment, the two share another sexually tense exchange.

"You're not going to actually kiss him?" I ask. "Are you?" I scoff. "You were just talking about my murder and now you're flirting?"

Drew laughs. "Not a date, I swear."

"Not a date?" Sarah repeats in a playful tone.

"It would be a date," I say, stating the obvious.

Sarah looks at her feet. Thankfully Drew moved the grey container to the back seat, otherwise it might have ruined the moment.

"Maybe we can do dinner," Sarah says and smiles. "It can be a date, if you want." She leaves the car.

Sarah closes the door and starts to walk inside the car rental building. Drew takes a few moments before he starts to leave the parking lot.

Before my sister enters the building she takes out her cell that's vibrating. She opens a text message from an unknown number.

"It's a date," the number says.

Sarah smiles and turns to look at Drew's car that's driving away. I begin to slowly clap at the exchange.

"Well done, Drew!" I shout. "The mortician has game. His game isn't... dead." I laugh hysterically at my joke, but my audience doesn't find it funny. "My talents are wasted," I say as I follow my sister into the building.

I look out the clear windows at Drew driving away. It seems my sister is just as infatuated with her ex-boyfriend as ever, but I have some questions.

One is, what in the name of everything that is good was in the grey box?

The second is, how did Drew arrive so quickly at my house after someone tried to break in?

CHAPTER 21

Sister

I walk through the front door of John's house. Alice is in the kitchen cooking something that smells heavenly. Melanie is in her craft area, furiously coloring a new piece of artwork.

Alice steps into the living room and grins. "Hey," she says. "Is that your ride? The car outside?"

I nod. "Yeah, I decided to rent a car for a few days. I didn't want to keep bothering you to use yours."

Alice waves me off. "Not a bother, Sarah," she says. "I almost wish you didn't rent one. Now I feel terrible that you're spending extra dollars that you didn't have to waste... What were you up to today?"

I take a deep breath and wonder how much I should say. "Well, I met up with someone for coffee."

"That's great," Alice says. "A friend?"

"Kind of. His name is Drew Picktin. Do you know him?"

Alice takes a moment before shaking her head when suddenly her eyes light up. "Wait, this is the Drew you dated, right? I think John mentioned his name before."

I give a thin smile. "Yeah, he was sort of a big deal back in the day for me."

Alice smirks. "Back in the day?" She laughs. "You make it sound like it happen ages ago. Did he ask you out or did you ask him?"

I smile. "I asked him."

Alice raises her eyebrows and makes an "ooo" sound. Melanie laughs from her craft room.

I didn't mention to Alice the reason I wanted to go out for coffee with him. I needed his opinion on whether a lamp base could be a murder weapon. Also, in my purse I have Mickey's diary. I have a night ahead of me of trying to find the dimensions of a lamp I bought years ago and reading what Mickey wrote.

"Is he single?" Alice asks.

"Uh, I'm not sure. I hope so given that he sort of asked me out on a date."

"Wasn't coffee with him a date?" Alice asks, confused.

"I'm not even sure how to describe what coffee was." I laugh.

Alice steps into the kitchen, grabs a spoon and stirs a pot on the oven. "Well, are you going to go on a date with him?"

I laugh. "I'm not sure. I thought about that when I was out renting a car. Feels like a weird time to reconnect with an ex."

Alice shakes her head. "Never a bad time if there's something to reconnect, in my opinion at least." She stirs the pot and stops the spoon. "Sorry, that must have come off weird. I know you're having a hard time. What I mean is, I met John during a messy- messy divorce. We made it work. If love is there, explore it."

I also want to point out that they met after my mom passed away from cancer, and that John and her knew each other, but bite my lip.

I nod. "I worry that we may end up down the same path we were on when we broke up. I'll be heading back to Toronto soon, and he'll be here with his cemetery."

"Cemetery?" Alice laughs.

I make a face. "Yeah, he's sort of a mortician now."

"You went on a date with a mortician?"

"Went out for coffee, actually," I say with a thin smile.

"Coffee," Melanie repeats with a deep tone as she scribbles on her page with a dark crayon.

Alice smiles at her daughter and looks at me. "Well, I still think it can't hurt to go on an actual date." She stirs her pot again. "Are you staying for dinner by the way? Or going back out?"

I step into the kitchen and take another whiff. "After smelling what you're cooking, I have to stay and eat, please."

"Of course," Alice says with a smile.

I think about what Drew revealed to me at our coffee "date". I still can't get over that he paid for Mickey's funeral himself.

"By the way," I whisper to Alice, "I'm very thankful you and John paid for Mickey's funeral, but I want to contribute as well. I want to pay you back."

Alice stops dead in her tracks. "John did what?"

My eyes widen. "He didn't tell you that?"

Alice takes a deep breath. "Yeah... no." She looks away and tries her best to keep her composure. "Thanks for telling me."

I'm going to feel bad for that one. I apologize to Alice again.

When I leave the kitchen, Melanie is still coloring

with a black crayon. "What are you working on?" I ask her.

"Hi, sister," she says as she continues to draw. "Car," she says, pointing at a weird shape on her page.

Inside the supposed car are five stick figures. I point at two of them that have what look like beaks. "I think I know what those are," I say with a laugh. "Penguins?"

"Penguins!" Melanie confirms enthusiastically.

I point at the stick figure that appears to be driving the car. "Is that your mom?"

Melanie nods. "Mom."

Finally, I look at the stick figure at the back of the car with spiky hair. "Who's that?" I ask. "Your dad?"

She shakes her head. "No," she says with a tone that makes me feel silly for asking, as though how can I not know who this stick figure is when it's obvious. "Mickey."

I look over her shoulder, taking in her picture. "Mickey," I say.

I wonder how much time Mickey spent with her. It was enough to leave an impression. She makes pictures with him alongside her beloved penguins. As I think of Mickey sitting with Melanie, the same as I'm doing now, a tear starts to form.

Melanie continues to color black outside the car. She stops suddenly and turns to me. "Sister, sad? Why?"

I take a deep breath and point at the spiky haired stick figure. "I miss my brother— *our* brother."

Melanie looks at me confused again. "Mickey, back." She points at her coloring page.

I turn my head and see Alice grabbing something from the fridge in the kitchen. When I look back at Melanie, I grab her hand softly. "No, sweetie. Mickey can't come back. He's gone. He's passed away. Do you understand, sweetie?"

She looks at me, confused. I'm about to try and explain it to her, something I'm sure John and Alice have been attempting to do as well, when she takes her picture and extends it towards me.

"Take," she says. "Take."

I smile. "You're giving me another piece of your artwork?" I ask her. When she smiles, I thank her and grab it.

"Not sad now?" she asks.

I give her a thin smile. "A little better, Melanie. Thanks, sister."

Melanie smiles at me as I leave her play area. When I get into the guest bedroom, I close the door behind me. I take out my brother's diary from my purse and stare at it.

Detective Drayson said his team processed the house, but I found a diary. I'm sure there won't be any major revelations that come to me if I read it, but I have to. After I do, I'll stop by the station and hand it to the authorities for evidence.

I can almost here Detective Drayson's voice. Don't expect much. It's not like Mickey would have written who killed him inside.

I need to read every word, though. I may pick up on something that maybe only I could see. Just like I did with the fake rock and the missing lamp.

I open the first page of the diary, and at the top, Mickey had written the date. He's only been using the journal for a few months, but Mickey wrote on nearly every page it seems.

On the first page, below the date, he wrote in bold letters: "Debt owed". On each line he has a name and the amount owed after. He owed nearly everyone something it seemed. He owed Jenn over a thousand. He owed his friends each a few hundred. He even had our biological father's name inside. Derrek Madson. At some point he owed our father nearly five hundred bucks, but he'd crossed the line off.

John's name is last on the list, and has the highest amount owed. Over fifteen thousand.

CHAPTER 22

Brother

Sarah examines the first page of my diary as I try to talk her out of it.

"No good shall come from this, sis," I try to explain. She continues to look at it anyway.

"How could you owe this much money?" she says as she looks at the numbers.

I lower my head, knowing how much I wrote and how little I paid back. "I had intentions to. Maybe I didn't. I'm not sure anymore... I wasn't trying to be that guy on purpose." I think of how upset John would be when we talked about money. "I wish I never asked for any of it."

Sarah had already mentioned selling the family home and using some of it to pay back John. That would make me happy, knowing that he'd get paid back, even if it wasn't directly from me.

After the fights I've had with John and knowing how upset Alice was with me over the money, knowing that in my death my debt was paid would make things somehow feel better. I hope she follows through with it. Knowing my sister, I know she will.

I didn't know John paid for my funeral as well. That was new information. I can't believe he would do that. I'm sure he knew that Sarah had no money, being a student.

I lower my head as I pace the guest room in my stepfather's house.

Seeing the charity of my stepfather reminds me of how terribly I messed up.

I wish I had done one thing right in the past few years of my life. It feels like it was failure after failure until someone put me out of my misery.

Sarah reads the date of the next entry. I quickly snap out of it as I realize what she's about to read.

"Sis!" I shout. "Put the book down!"

Sarah makes a face as she reads my words out loud. "Today I banged Jenn Harring six times," she reads in disgust. She shakes her head and continues reading. "I could have gone a few more times but Jenn was the one who couldn't continue LOL." She lets out an audible sigh. "Seriously, Mickey?"

I shake my head. "I told you. No good shall come from this." Sarah lowers my journal and I feel relieved. For a change she's listening to me, although I'm sure it's the words I wrote when I was living that deterred her from reading on.

She opens her laptop and starts typing in searches.

"What are we doing now?" I ask Sarah. She types in "lamps" on Google and searches through the shopping page. "You're looking for the lamp. You'll be at this all night."

I sit beside her on the bed, looking over her shoulder as she searches. When I breathe out near her, she waves her hand near her hair as if I'm a fly.

"Sorry," I say, realizing I'm a little too close.

"Where did we get that stupid lamp from?" Sarah asks out loud.

I turn to her. "Seriously? You forgot?" I laugh. "How could you? Don't you remember how we found the lamp?"

Sarah continues to search. She doesn't do well hiding her frustration at her inability to remember where we got the lamp from.

I put my hands on top of her shoulder. "Don't give up, sis," I say. "I know you'll remember. We were looking on so many sites to try and find her a gift until I typed in a search, 'what gift should we buy our mom when we can't think for ourselves'. The lamp website was the first to pop up."

Sarah raises her head. "Mickey searched something stupid," she says with a thin smile. She starts typing what I wrote years ago and narrows her search. The site we bought the lamp from is no longer top of the search results but is now third.

Sarah smiles as she and I read the description of the lamp.

"This hand-painted, durable and heavy cast iron lamp will bring any room to life with its beauty."

I shake my head in disbelief. If Sarah's right, it certainly did not bring life to my living room. It definitely was heavy and durable, though. I'm sure the manufacturer won't add how many times you can strike someone with the lamp without it breaking in the description.

"I knew you could do it," I tell her.

"Yes!" Sarah says out loud.

If I could, I'd give her a high five. Sarah takes out her cell phone and takes a picture of the store where you can purchase it. She makes a phone call and gives an audible sigh when it goes straight to voicemail.

She leaves another message for Detective Drayson,

telling him she believes she has an idea what the object is that may have been used in my murder. After getting off the phone, she texts him with a picture of the lamp.

Immediately she opens a new text message. I don't have to look over her shoulder to see who it is to, but I do anyway.

"Hey, Drew," she types. She attaches a photo of the lamp, adding a separate photo that shows its dimensions and asks if he believes this could have been what was used.

Drew must have been waiting for my sister all day to text him as he replies immediately before Sarah can even lower her phone.

"I'll look into it and talk to you soon," he replies. Immediately after, he sends a winking emoji.

I roll my eyes. "Sis, I really don't understand what you see in this guy."

"Thanks again," she types back.

Sarah lowers her phone and looks at my diary again.

"Can we not look at my most intimate thoughts again?" I plead. Again, my stubborn sister picks it up and starts looking through its pages. "Here we go again," I say. "Tell me if you find something interesting."

I pace around the room as she reads on, thinking about what I've learned myself today. Even though Sarah can't hear me, at times I think she feels my presence. She waves me off when I get too close to her.

Then there's the big revelation at my house.

I wasn't able to leave Sarah's line of sight when we were at my house and someone was at the door. I was physically unable to leave the room where she was as if something, some force was holding me back.

It dawns on me as well that I don't remember what

happened to me prior to Sarah returning to Pinewood Springs. I don't even remember what happens when she falls asleep. I don't watch over her or anything weird like that.

The afterlife for me isn't wearing cutout sheets, making spooky sounds and freaking people out when they sleep. The only time I exist is when my sister is awake. When she's not, I'm not sure where I go or what happens.

The idea of that freaks me out.

Sarah sits up in the bed. "What did you find now?" I ask.

I peer over her shoulder. It's a page of me talking about breaking things off with Jenn. Even months ago, I knew being with her would only make things worse for me.

We were toxic together. Gave each other permission to continue using. I knew one of us had to end things permanently, otherwise we'd continue until one of us was in an early grave.

Too late for me, of course. Forty-one blows... using the lamp my sister and I bought my mom. The idea of my murder is making me more and more sad.

Sarah found what she was looking for. Confirmation that I was going to end things permanently. I like to think that the night I was killed, I meant it too. Little did I know that it could be the reason I'm in my current state.

I shake my head as I think of my girlfriend. How could she do this to me?

CHAPTER 23

Sister

I pull up to the house my GPS gives me for Jenn's address. Besides being a sex diary, my brother managed to give me some useful insights through his journal.

The amount owed to people in his circle was interesting. Continuous mentions of Woods Bar and Grill, where him and his friends would drink were also noteworthy. The details about him wanting to break things off with Jenn in the last few pages of his journal had me thinking.

Thankfully, he even provided me with her address. I'm not sure why my brother wrote her address in his book. It was scribbled at the bottom of one of the pages with her name beside it.

Luckily, this may be her house.

I walk up the steps of her wooden porch and knock on the door. When it opens, an older woman with frizzy dark hair answers.

"Can I help you?" she asks.

"Hi, is Jenn home?" I say, peeking behind her.

She looks me up and down for a moment. "No, she just left for work... Are you friends?" She raises an eyebrow.

"No," I say. "My name's Sarah. I'm Mickey Roland's sister."

She purses her lips when I say Mickey's name. I've seen a look like this before. Sometimes, when I thought of my brother, when he was alive, I had the same expression. I can only imagine what this woman, who I can only assume is Jenn's mother, is thinking.

"I'm sorry for your loss," she says.

"Thanks. Will Jenn be coming home later?"

She sighs. "I never know where or what my daughter will be up to, so no, sorry." She closes the door slightly. "I'll tell her you came."

As I thank her, she shuts the door. I head to my car and wonder why Jenn's mom felt so tense with me. Was it simply because I was Mickey's sister? With them breaking it off and back on so often and his history of using, I'm sure she had more than a few conversations with her daughter about my brother.

I also can't help but be frustrated. I travelled over an hour to get here and, of course, Jenn's not home. Just my luck.

I start to drive down the road. After a few blocks, I see a bus stop ahead and a slender woman with blond hair waiting. It's Jenn Harring.

Seems like my luck has changed.

I roll down my window and drive up to the bus stop. "Hey, Jenn," I say to her with a smile. She looks at me confused. "It's Sarah. We met the other day. I'm Mickey's sister."

"I know," she says. "Uh... hi."

"Want a ride?" I ask.

She looks around. "No, I'm fine. My bus will be coming soon."

"You sure? I can give you a ride to work," I tell her. "I'm sure it will be quicker than public transit... and less smelly."

Now she looks even more puzzled. "How did you know I was going to work?"

"Your mom told me," I say. "I just came from your house."

She shakes her head. "How did you even know where I live? Never mind, I'm fine. It was nice to see you. Have a good day."

"I was hoping we could talk today. About Mickey."

"What about him?" she asks.

"At the funeral I said I wanted to get to know more about what he was like. I feel like I didn't know him well near the end."

She takes a deep breath. "You can't park here," she says.

I pull my car up and park a little further down the road. I quickly get out and run up to Jenn. "Sorry, I know you're busy, but I need to know about my brother."

She looks at me wide eyed. "It's better that you don't. Things were bad. They're still bad for me. Look, what do you want me to tell you? We got high all the time. Okay? Now you know."

I let out a heavy breath, realizing this is not going the way I wanted. Worse, I see a bus heading our way.

"Can we meet up later for coffee? My treat. Like I said, I just want to get to know my brother better through you."

"No thanks," she says curtly. As the bus pulls up to the stop, the doors open. She looks at me coldly. "Please stop following me around."

Before she steps on the bus, I shout at her, "Why are

you staying quiet to the cops? What did you do?"

Jenn looks back at me for a moment before continuing to sweep her transit pass on the machine, ignoring me. I watch as she heads towards the back of the bus.

"Hey!" the driver shouts at me. I turn to him. "Getting on or what?"

I shake my head and look at Jenn Harring, who sits on the opposite side of the bus from me, gazing out the window.

CHAPTER 24

Sister

I park outside the Woods Bar and Grill. The lot is nearly empty except for a beat-up Volkswagen and a red truck. As I look at the truck, my mind races to the other night when a truck was following me down an empty road.

Is this the same?

I step out of my car and look at the truck. I can't help but notice the rear bumper sticker, which reads "I Love Bitches".

Mickey's journal said that him and his friends hung out here often. With any luck, his friends will be here. Seeing the truck, I'm also worried that it belongs to them. My gut is telling me it does, and I believe it.

Some real classy friends you've made, Mickey. Who were you running around with before you were murdered?

The bar itself looks nearly dilapidated. It's located just outside town near the highway. If I was driving by, I'd assume it was shut down. Out of all the letters on the front of the bar, only the second last "O" and "D" lights are functional. What should read as "Woods Bar and Grill" in the dark only says "O D".

No wonder the bar is empty.

When I enter, things go from bad to worse. None of the furniture appears clean or without tears. I believe I see one chair that's broken on the floor for some reason. The bar reeks of beer and other odd odours.

It's easy to spot Mickey's friends, Jake Matthews and Lenny Mercer, by the bar, laughing between themselves. Close by is a man drinking alone on the other side of the bar. Then there's the bartender himself. There's only us four here.

As I walk in, Lenny's booming voice stops laughing and Jake whispers something to him. The bartender stops filling the fridge with bottled beer, stands and looks at me. Even the man drinking alone turns his head slightly toward me before going back to his glass.

I wonder how many times a female has stepped inside this establishment.

"Can I help you?" the bartender asks with a surprised look on his face that reads, "I don't make cosmos."

"I think she's with us," Jake says with a grin. "Mickey's sister, right?"

"Yeah, hey," I say to him. "I was hoping to talk to you guys."

Lenny scoffs. "Well, you're smart enough to know where to find us." He laughs. "I guess we're pretty easy to locate on Saturday night."

Jake shakes his head. "It's Monday night, stupid."

Lenny laughs again. "Right." He takes his massive hands and wraps them around his beer, making the bottle look like it's for a child, and drinks until it's empty.

"Want a beer?" Jake asks me. He puts his hands through his short brown hair. He too grabs his beer bottle with his equally large hands. These two men look like they wrestle bears when they're not drinking their faces off.

"What about a shot?" Jake says.

"I'm okay," I say. "I was hoping to talk to you guys."

"Yeah, we know," Lenny says, "you already said that." He laughs.

Jake pushes him and Lenny shoves him back. Lenny's eyes fill with rage for a moment until Jake whispers something to him.

"Well, we can't have much of a conversation with you that far away," Jake says. Lenny smiles and shakes his head.

I reluctantly step towards them. As I do, the grins on their faces somehow look even more menacing than before. My gut is telling me to leave. If I were to see these two men in a dark alley, I'd run and scream, but I'm in a public bar. There's at least two other people here. I'm sure it's safe enough for me to talk to them.

A sense of dread washes over me suddenly. It's as if a voice inside me is telling me to go. Don't talk to them. Just leave.

They own the red truck. Somehow I know it. It's a fifty-fifty chance it's their vehicle and I don't think the truck belongs to the aging old man drinking alone. The bumper sticker on the truck doesn't seem to match the old man's personality.

"Three tequila shots," Jake says to the bartender, who nods back at him.

"Tequila?" Lenny says, making a sour face.

"Come on," Jake says, pushing him playfully this time. "For Mickey. We got his sister with us. It's only right we have his favourite shot."

Lenny takes a deep breath followed by a loud burp.

"Sure. For Mickey."

As the bartender pours the shots, Lenny leers at me and Jake smiles. Jake shoves a shot towards his friend and picks up the other two, extending one glass towards me.

"For your brother," he says. "May he... rest in peace."

I look at the tiny glass in his massive hand. I'm not sure if it's the stinky bar, the fact that they own a red truck, my guess that the glass hasn't been properly cleaned, or the men themselves, but something about Jake and Lenny feels off. Again, my gut is screaming at me to leave here.

Somehow, I know without having to be told that these men are dangerous. The type of men that could put something in my drink if I wasn't watching.

"I'm okay," I say. "Thanks, though. I was hoping to talk to you guys about my brother."

Jake keeps his hand extended towards me even though I've refused. "For your brother. First shot on me."

Lenny laughs. "Yeah, and then Mickey's sister can pick up the tab after." Jake stares at his friend and he shuts up immediately.

In the moment, and out of fear, I nearly take the drink. Instead, I stare at Jake's eyes. They're cold, and a chill runs down my spine. He may have a smile on his face, but his eyes are telling me something different. I've never seen someone look so angry and smile.

"No," I say again, this time turning my body away from him.

When it becomes apparent that I will not take a drink from them, Jake's grin quickly leaves his face and for a moment I feel he shows his true colors as we share a brief exchange. His dead eyes somehow become even more glossed over than before.

How many drinks have these two had tonight?

Jake turns to Lenny and the two raise their shot glasses. "To Mickey," Jake says. The two of them put their heads back and down the shot.

Lenny makes another sour face. "Hate tequila, ugh." Lenny grabs the third shot out of Jake's hand. He looks at me and raises the drink. "To Mickey's sister!" He laughs before popping his large neck back and downing the drink.

Every ounce of my being is screaming at me to leave these men alone. I can't, though. I need to know.

"I was hoping you guys could tell me about my brother," I say to them. "What happened before he was—"

"Killed," Lenny says, finishing my statement. He looks at Jake and back at me. "Didn't you already get the story from Jenn?" He laughs.

How did they know I spoke with Jenn?

Jake smirks at me. "She texted us. She gave us the heads up you may be showing up."

Lenny nods. "So, what, you're going around playing detective with Mickey's friends? Trying to figure out who killed him? You think it was us?" He laughs.

Jake looks at him a moment before smiling at me. "Well, look, we're about to leave. We're heading back to my place. Come with us. We'll talk some more. I'll tell you all about Mickey."

"All about Mickey, sure," Lenny agrees.

"Where do you live?" I ask. I can hear a voice inside me shouting again. *What am I doing? Why would I even give them the idea that I'd be willing to go to their place?*

"It's a bit tricky to explain," Jake says.

"Easier if you just hop in the truck with us," Lenny says.

Jake gives me a thin smile. "I'll drop you back off here when you want."

Lenny laughs. "You can question us all night." For a moment, his eyes gaze at my chest. I feel the urge to fold my arms across my body but thankfully he looks away.

"No, that's okay," I tell them. "I'm just going to go."

"You didn't even get a chance to talk to us about your brother," Jake says.

"Yeah," Lenny says with a surprised tone. "I thought you were going to keep pretending you're a copper with us." He puts up his pointer finger at me and makes gunshot noises.

"I just want to know what happened to Mickey," I say. "That's all."

Jake nods. "Of course. You're, like, trying to solve what happened." He puts a hand to his chest. "If I had a little sister and something terrible happened to her, I'd do the same thing."

"Yeah," Lenny says. "Same here. Besides, Mickey told us how smart you are."

Jake smirks. "Let's go back to my place and put our heads together. Figure this out." Lenny turns to me and smiles, and my insides turn again. I feel nauseous.

The old man at the bar hasn't paid the three of us any attention, but the bartender's expression is different. His eyes are wide as he watches our exchange. It's as if I can read his thoughts.

Don't you dare go with them.

For a change, I listen to my gut and stop being so stubborn. "It's starting to get late," I say. "Thanks for the offer though."

"Another time," Jake says. "We'll see you soon."

Lenny laughs. "I think she's nervous around us, Jake."

Jake shakes his head in response. "Too bad. We could have helped."

I turn to leave but Lenny calls out to me. "If we think of anything about the case, copper, we'll come by your stepdad's house and talk to you."

I turn to him, my eyes wide and full of fear. How does he know where I'm staying?

I take a few steps back toward the exit as Jake smiles at me. "Have a good night."

CHAPTER 25

Brother

As my sister drives away from the bar, I continuously look in the side mirror to ensure there's no red truck behind us.

Thankfully, Jake or Lenny isn't following us tonight.

Thankfully, my sister had the common sense to get out of that bar and away from my so-called friends.

The thought of what they did to my sister just now infuriates me. They could easily kick my ass, but had I been alive and they pulled that crap with Sarah, it would be worth getting beat up over.

How could they talk to her that way?

I always knew they were not great people, but we called ourselves friends. As tough as they were, when the drugs and alcohol kicked in, they could be vulnerable, like me. They'd tell me their problems and I'd share mine.

I considered them like brothers at one time.

To think that's how they were with my sister makes me wonder how much I really knew either of them. It's almost like I knew none of the people I thought were important in my life.

Jake, Lenny and Jenn. Now that I'm dead and have a clear mind, I don't understand what I saw in any of them.

A beam of light from a vehicle behind us makes me tense up. When I look back, I see a small car and feel immediate relief.

"Please tell me we're going home, sis," I tell Sarah. As we drive down John's street, my tension eases.

We walk into John's house and he's on the couch, alone, watching television. He stands up to greet Sarah.

"Hey, I was wondering if you were going to come back tonight," he says.

"Yeah," Sarah answers, "I was out longer than I expected. Alice and Melanie are asleep already?"

He raises his eyebrows. "Yes, and I got the impression that I should take my time coming to bed tonight." He lets out a laugh. "I should have told Alice about paying for the funeral. It was dumb of me to keep that secret."

"I'm sorry I mentioned it," Sarah says. "I didn't know. I didn't even think about payment for a funeral. My head's been spinning since finding out about Mickey."

John shakes his head. "Not your fault, at all. It's mine."

"Why did you pay for his funeral?" Sarah asks.

John's mouth lowers and if anyone could see me, I'm sure I wouldn't be able to hide my expression at her direct question either. I have to admit, I'm just as curious.

"Well," he says, trying to find the words. "I don't know. It felt right, I suppose. I mean, I lived in that house with your mother, you and Michael for such a long time... It just felt right. I know you probably wouldn't have money to help since you're in school."

Sarah face lightens as he explains. "I know he owes you a bunch of money as well."

John smiles. "Yeah, he did."

"I want to pay you back. I'm planning on selling

the house and after that, I want to pay you back for everything he owed, plus the funeral costs."

John puts up a hand. "That's really nice of you, Sarah. Please, let me pay for the funeral, though."

Sarah's eyes narrow as she stares at him. Even I look at my stepfather as he says it.

John smiles. "I know you're just as stubborn as your mom was, but please, let me pay for the funeral. It's the least I can do for Mickey... It would make your mom happy if she knew I had. The idea of that makes me happy as well. I want you to know that I still think of her often."

Sarah lowers her head. "Thanks, John."

"Sure," he says.

I take in his words. It hits me how much John cared for me, even though I wasn't his biological son. "Thanks, John," I say to him as well. "Thanks for everything."

"So," John says with raised eyebrows, "you and Drew Picktin again, huh?"

Sarah laughs. "It was just coffee."

I laugh. "It was extremely awkward is what it was. Thankfully you didn't have to be there as well, John."

"I'm happy to hear though," he says. "Drew always seemed like a decent guy."

Sarah nods. "Well, I'm going to go to bed. Thanks again, John. For everything. Thanks for opening your house to me."

"Of course," John says. He puts a finger up. "Wait, before you go, I promised to give you this." He walks into the kitchen and comes back with a stack of papers. The top page has several stick figures on it.

I smile to myself, noticing who the artist is.

"Melanie made these for you," he says to Sarah. Sarah takes the pile and nearly drops a page.

"So many." She grins.

"Yeah," John says. "She says you were sad, and she wanted to cheer you up with her artwork. Heads up, many of them are penguins. My favorite was of you, her and two penguins all holding hands." He chuckles. "She says you four were doing the 'happy dance'."

I laugh with him. Melanie is the best. I peek at one of the papers that slipped out of the pile onto the floor. There has to be at least twenty penguins surrounding the stick figure girl in the middle. I'm pretty sure Melanie would love to have her own army of penguins someday.

Sarah laughs nearly as hard as me. "She is such a sweetheart."

John smiles back. "She likes having you around. You may need to buy another suitcase before you leave just for her artwork." He momentarily looks serious. "By the way, don't feel bad about not keeping them. Just maybe throw them away outside the house. I made the mistake of tossing one in the kitchen garbage and Melanie got so upset when she found it. She still checks the trash sometimes to ensure we haven't thrown out her artwork."

Sarah and John exchange goodnights. Once inside her room, she slips into the bedsheets and stares at the ceiling.

I can only imagine what she's thinking. She's done so much in a single day. Went to our family home, spoke with Jenn and Lenny and Jake.

I know she wants to figure out what happened to me. I can see how hard she's trying to piece it together.

But if it ends up putting her in the way of people like Jake and Lenny, I'd rather she leave town. Go back to university. I paid for my lifestyle with my own life. If something were to happen to my sister because she was snooping around too much, I couldn't handle it.

Just as like the night before, I know once she's asleep, I won't be here again until she wakes up. Or maybe I won't come back at all.

My existence is tied to my twin sister.

"I miss you," Sarah whispers as she stares blankly at the ceiling.

I can feel her emotions inside her. I feel the love she has for me. An image of us as kids hits me. When we were five, Mom had us share a bedroom for the convenience of putting us to sleep at the same time. Sometimes when she'd leave our room, I'd wake up and be completely scared to death.

I was such a scaredy cat, as the saying goes. I laugh, thinking about how afraid I was when I was young.

Every time I woke up scared, I'd wake up Sarah. Even though she was older than me by minutes, she took to the role of being oldest sibling well. She would comfort me by kissing my forehead and holding me until I drifted to sleep.

She was always there for me. Even now that my physical body is gone, she's here for me still.

"I miss you too, Sarah," I say to her. Of course, she doesn't hear my words. I hope she can feel them though. The past few days there have been times I know she could.

I hope she knows how much I love her. How much I miss her. How much I wish I wasn't such a screw-up in life before it ended for me.

Sarah closes her eyes. I stand over her bed and wish her goodnight. I lower my head to hers.

"Thanks for being there for me," I whisper in her ear. I kiss her forehead. "I love you."

I'm about to leave when Sarah suddenly sits up in bed. "Mickey?" she says.

My eyes light up. "Yes! It's me. I'm here."

Sarah shakes her head and looks towards the window that she left open. She gets out of bed and quickly closes it before getting back inside the sheets.

I smile at her. "Goodnight, Sarah."

CHAPTER 26
Sister

I spent the morning making my own artwork with Melanie as John and Alice got ready for their day.

John skipped breakfast and shot out the door, saying he needed to get extra work done at the hardware store today. Alice got herself dolled up after breakfast.

Mornings are hectic in this house. It's nice taking time off university. I put so much pressure on myself to keep up my high grades that I wish I could slow things down and just color. Drawing with Melanie is so therapeutic.

I should do it more often.

Hitting the pause button on life to grieve for my brother hasn't been what I thought it would be. I assumed I'd be a hot mess with a lot of ugly-crying and snot-clearing.

Instead, I've been busy playing Nancy Drew. If I didn't have that, I'd have to face how emotionally broken I feel. Playing detective seems more fun.

Melanie puts down a crayon and hands me her latest masterpiece. I examine the stick figures inside a house. In the oddly shaped building is a character I've seen before, Alice. Then Melanie and me. All three of us are holding hands.

This time she didn't draw Mickey, thankfully.

Just as I play detective to escape my emotions, I wonder if Melanie uses her artwork to help manage her own feelings. I wonder if her pictures are how she grieves. In some way she must know that Mickey is not coming back. As she continues to make more art, will I see less and less of a spikey-haired stick figure that represents my brother?

Well, *our* brother, I suppose.

She didn't draw John in this picture, which I find surprising. Come to think of it, she hasn't drawn him in any of the pictures she's given me.

"Thanks, sister," I say to her, looking at the picture she made. Melanie beams as she starts making another. "Wait." She looks at me. I hand her a picture I've made this time. "It's for you." I point at the two stick figures that are standing under a smiley face sun. "That's us." I point at the green grass I made. "We're about to have a picnic."

You wouldn't know that, looking at my picture. Sadly, my creative side is not as strong as the analytical part of me.

"Thanks, sister!" she says enthusiastically. Her wide smile somehow grows larger as she wraps her hands around my midsection. I laugh and I'm curiously amazed at her strength as she does.

"You're welcome."

"Melanie!" Alice calls as she walks across the living room toward the front door. "Time to go. We're going to be late for school."

"Aw!" Melanie pouts. She looks at me and at her mother. "No school!" she shouts. "Sister here."

Alice takes a deep breath.

I put my hand up to her. "It's okay," I say to Alice. I turn to Melanie. "Everyone has to go to school, sister. We'll make more pictures together when you come home, okay?"

"Promise?" Melanie asks.

I nod. "Promise."

Alice rushes her daughter to get ready to leave. Moments later, I have the house to myself.

Another day in my small hometown. After what happened with Mickey's friends, I wonder if continuing to play Nancy Drew alone is a smart idea.

Being in their presence frightened me. I've never felt that way around anyone.

My cell buzzes in my pocket. I quickly take it out and see it's from an unknown number.

"Hello?" I say when I answer.

"It's Detective Drayson," the officer says. "I just wanted to give you a call back to let you know I'll have our forensics guy look into the lamp. Sorry, I meant to get back to you sooner. It's just been insanely busy. I'll be coming back to Pinewood Springs tonight."

I take a deep breath, relieved that he called. I was worried he was ignoring my attempts to reach him. "Thanks, Detective."

"Again, I'm sorry. Are you staying in town much longer?"

"I don't have plans to leave," I tell him. I lower my head. "I'm not sure I can until I know what happened to Mickey."

There's a brief pause. "This isn't easy," he tells me. "I've met with many family members of people who were brutally taken away from them. Staying in town, waiting for answers, won't make it easier for you... if you want, I can ask our social worker to speak with you. She's great. Very helpful."

I don't answer him. Instead, I focus on my brother and what I think could be clues I found yesterday. I tell him about the missing key and picture frame. He says he may have his team go back out to the house to examine it again.

I also mention the diary I found. I explain how I found it in a special hiding place in Mickey's room. He asks me to drop it off at the station today. I tell him I would, but first, I'll be taking some pictures of its content for my own investigation.

"You said you found him, my brother's body, in Pinewood Springs Park, right?"

I can almost visualize the officer rolling his eyes at me dismissing him. "That's right. His body was found along the river by a hiker."

"Okay," I say. I think of Jake and Lenny. "I ended up speaking with Mickey's friends last night at a bar."

"Do you mean Jake Matthews and Lenny Mercer?"

"Yeah," I confirm. "When I asked them about Mickey, they scared me."

"Did they threaten you?" the detective asks. "What did they say?"

"Not directly, no. They definitely intimidated me, asking me to come to their place to talk about Mickey."

This time I audibly hear the detective let out a heavy breath. "I know you want to find out what happened to your brother. I understand that, I do, but you can't be talking to people like that alone. Your brother did not keep good company. You are not safe around them. These are the type of men that if I had to charge them with a crime, I'd bring a squad to aid in the arrest. Please, promise me that you won't speak to them again."

I sigh in response.

"Investigations take time, Sarah," the detective continues. "It will continue for a long time. Even if we have all the evidence we need to convict someone, it takes a while to put all the pieces of what we need together before an arrest occurs. If you're staying in Pinewood Springs to wait until you find closure, that will take a long time."

I let out a breath, taking in his words. "What about my brother?" I ask.

"What do you mean?"

"Was he like his friends?" As I say the words, I realize how little I knew about Mickey before he was killed.

There's a pause on the phone. "No violent convictions, no. Mickey did have one conviction for possession of illicit drugs. He wasn't known for being a tough guy like his friends. I didn't know him to be violent in nature."

I take a deep breath. "The night of Mickey's funeral, I think a truck was following me after I spoke with you. I think it was Mickey's friends. A red truck was behind me as I drove. When I turned, the truck followed."

"Did you see one of them driving?" the detective asks.

"No," I say. "I only remember the red truck. When I went to the bar last night to talk to them, I saw what I thought looked like the same one."

"You are not certain, though?" the detective asks.

"No," I say again. "Yesterday, too, when I was inside my family home, someone tried to break in. They even went to the back door to try and enter. I didn't see who it was. I was too scared."

Detective Drayson is quiet a moment. "You need to be careful," he tells me.

I thank the detective for calling me back before ending the call. I know what he says makes sense. Why stay in town any longer?

I'm searching for my brother's killer in a small town. I need to be careful, the detective told me. But I also need answers.

There were other people my brother got money from. I need to talk to all of them, no matter how much I hate it.

CHAPTER 27

Brother

"Thanks for meeting with me," Sarah says as she sits in the small lunchroom.

Across from her sits none other than our father, our biological one. John shared where he worked with Sarah. What Sarah doesn't know is John and Mom only found out where our dad was living because he owed back childcare and refused to pay. A judge ordered him to.

"I wish I knew you wanted to reach out," Derrek Madson says. "We could have, I don't know, gone out for dinner."

Sarah gives a thin smile. "That would be nice. Maybe another time."

My father leans back in his chair, taking another bite of his sandwich. I was surprised to find out he's a production manager at the factory. I didn't think he was capable of leading since he could never manage his own life... or his children.

A production manager at a factory that makes toys for children. The irony of this is not lost on me. I can only imagine what Sarah thought when she walked into the facility and read the information about the company as she waited for the receptionist to get our dad.

His higher-ups allowed him to take an early break to speak to Sarah.

Derrek smiles. "You know, it's funny. When you were born, everyone thought you looked just like your mother. After all, Mickey did. Even I'll admit that. I never saw it, though, with you. I always thought you took after me, and I think I was right. Now that you're an adult yourself, I see it plain as day."

I roll my eyes. They do seem to bear a strong resemblance, but thankfully, personality makes a big difference.

"Last I heard from your mom, you were leaving to go to university," he says.

Sarah nods. "Yeah, I'm taking criminology at the U of T. I only have a year left."

Derrek smiles. "Wow, my own daughter, a university graduate."

I laugh as I watch them. I walk up to another man who's spooning some soup in his mouth at a table behind them. "Can you believe this guy?" I say to the stranger. "It's like he's pretending he had some hand in my sister's accomplishments."

"You know," our father continues, "you'll be the only one on my side of the family that has a university degree. That's something."

"Thanks," Sarah says.

I'm taken aback by how quiet and timid my sister seems. I remind myself she hasn't seen our father since she was a kid. She likely didn't even remember what he looked like until today.

"So, I take it you're here because of Michael," he says.

I sigh. "Mickey, you bastard."

"Yeah," Sarah replies. "I'm not sure how long I'll be

staying."

"Well, I'm glad you came to see me," he says. "I sometimes wondered what kind of a woman you turned out to be and I have to say, I'm proud of the results."

Sarah fidgets in her chair. "I was hoping to talk to you about Mickey."

He smiles. "What about him?"

"I know you two met up a few times," she says. "I'm curious what happened."

A man walks into the room and apologizes for interrupting us. "Sorry, boss," he says, shoving a clipboard in front of Derrek. "Just need you to sign off on this order."

"Yeah, no worries," Derrek says, signing it. Sarah leans in and looks at his signature as he does. The man leaves and Derrek smiles at Sarah again.

"You want to know what happened when Michael and I met? He reached out to me out of nowhere one day. I think it was your stepfather who gave him my contact info. Jim."

"John," Sarah corrects him.

"Right, John." He wipes his mouth with a napkin. "Well, Michael came, and we talked a little. It was upsetting to see how he was. He didn't look well."

"He wasn't," my sister confirms.

"Right," Derrek says. "We talked a few times, and he stopped coming around. Then I found out about his death."

"Murder," Sarah corrects him again.

Derrek lets out a laugh in response to Sarah's tone after being corrected so many times. "It was terrible, of course. I wish I could have done more for him."

"What about the money?" Sarah asks.

"Money?" Derrek repeats.

"Mickey asked you for money, right?"

Derrek nods. "He did. A couple hundred bucks. He paid me back. He asked for more. I said no. Then he stopped showing up. I saw quickly what he wanted from me."

Sarah shakes her head and I see her bite her lip. I know my sister. She's about to erupt and our poor father will feel it. Instead, Sarah keeps it in.

"And that's it?" Sarah asks.

"That's it," Derrek confirms. He takes a deep breath. "I sense that you're angry at me. Maybe this wasn't a good idea."

"*Angry*?" Sarah says. "I'm furious. Your only son dies, and you can't be bothered to go to his funeral."

"I went… after," he says with a harsh tone. He makes a gesture for her to lower her voice. "I did go to his grave," he says, lighter. "When no one was around, I paid my respects to him." He leans back. "I was sorry that he ended up that way."

"Sorry," Sarah says, her eyes staring blankly. "It was you who left the note at his grave?"

He looks at her strangely. "That was my note, yes."

"What are you sorry for?" Sarah asks.

"What?" Derrek says, confused.

Sarah rolls her eyes at our father's response. "What did you do that warrants an apology? One that you handwrote and left on your murdered son's grave?"

He suddenly looks disgusted. "What are you trying to say to me?"

"Are you sorry because you did something to him? Hurt him? Or sorry for being a trash father your whole life?"

My eyes widen as my sister tears into our father.

Even the soup guy momentarily puts down his spoon to listen in.

"What was I going to do when my junkie son knocks on my door begging for money?" Derrek snaps back. "I refused him the second time he asked. I wondered if I should have just given him what he wanted." He points a finger at Sarah. "Now don't you dare tell me I'm somehow responsible for what happened to Michael."

"Mickey," Sarah snaps back. "He went by Mickey. Only Mom called him Michael."

I can feel the rage inside my sister build, and I'm here for it. I'm cheerleading it on from the sideline. I wish I could join in.

"I'm his father," he says. "I named him Michael."

Sarah scoffs. "Why do you think he wanted to go by Mickey instead?" She laughs. "And *father*? I don't think so. You're just the sperm donor who helped create us."

The man at the other table spits out his soup and holds his mouth, trying to hold back his laughter. Derrek looks at him and he quickly quiets.

Our father looks back at my sister. "I work here," he says. "You can't talk to me like that here. I think we're done."

Sarah stands up. "That's right. Raincheck on that dinner with daddy. I think you were right before. It's better I don't know you."

Sarah lets her word sink into my father's chest before she leaves. The man at the other table tries his best to continue eating his soup.

CHAPTER 28
Sister

I turn off the highway onto a gravel road passing a sign that reads "Pinewood Springs National Park".

When I park my rental car in the empty lot, I step outside and take in the wilderness around me. There are a handful of national parks in Alberta, and while Pinewood Springs's is the smallest, it still covers a vast wilderness with many trails.

Only a few, though, go by the river where Mickey's body was found.

I used to love it here. Mickey and I came here often with Mom when we were kids. She'd take us on mini hikes for a few hours, as much as children can handle without crying and wanting to go back home to their video games.

When we were older, she'd bring us on longer trips. My favourite trail was one that led to a small waterfall that took nearly two hours to get to. It was gorgeous there. I remember when Drew and I first started dating, he had never been to the falls. We took a day and went together, having sandwiches that Drew made once we finally got there.

So many fond memories of this area growing up, but now they're tainted forever, knowing that my brother's body was found in these woods.

As beautiful as the area is, there's usually no one here. I can see why the killer hid his body here.

Detective Drayson said Mickey's body was found by a hiker along the river. There's only a handful of trails near the river, which narrows it down. Only one is closest to the parking lot, though.

A large map is underneath a small, roofed area. I take a moment to read it to find where I'm going.

I find the trail easily, but before I start hiking, I take a moment to look at another trail, the one that leads to the falls. At least that memory won't be tainted.

An image of my brother's mangled body hits me. An image of what it must have looked like to discover his corpse in these woods. My mind has a sinister sense of humor to think of something so terrible, but maybe it's my conscience telling me I shouldn't be here.

Terrible things have happened here.

I should just leave, but I'm determined. I'm determined to find out the truth. My brother needs to rest in peace. My mind needs to find peace again. Until my brother's murderer is discovered, I'm not able to rest.

Mickey called me, asking for help, the night he was killed.

I've made a promise to help him, even though he wasn't alive when I answered him.

As I walk along the trail, I think of more fond memories I have growing up. Mother raised us by herself, until John came into the picture. After meeting my real dad, John is a saint in comparison. I had reservations about him when Mom brought him into our life. She said she had been dating him for nearly six months before bringing him around Mickey and me.

I hated the idea of that when I was a kid. It was like our mom had a secret life with a man she never told us about. Of course, now that I'm older, I understand that she didn't want to bring around every boyfriend she may have had. Still, I wish I could go back in time and appreciate the type of person John is.

He was part of a lot of loving memories, even though he wasn't my real father. Now he has a new daughter, Melanie. Even though he isn't Melanie's real father, he loves her just as much as Alice does.

Unlike me when I was her age, Melanie loves John. Staying at his house the past few days just confirms it.

The man may have no children of his own, but he's fathered many.

I never knew what my real father was like. I had many assumptions. None of my thoughts ended up being the reality. Telling off the stranger who called himself my father felt good in the moment. I do wish I'd got him to say more. I couldn't help myself, though. As Derrek spoke, each of his words disgusted me.

When he talked down about Mickey, I couldn't stop myself from telling him off. At least I discovered who the note belonged to. That's one mystery solved.

I look around the trail. At some point, it follows the river. If I were a murderer, I wouldn't have dragged a corpse too far. The river is somewhere off-trail nearby. I just have to find it. Thankfully, I do hear the distant sounds of flowing water.

I step off the trail toward the sounds. After taking a few steps, the sound of a branch snapping behind me causes me to turn my head.

"Hello?" I yell. I'm not sure if I'm hearing things or just hypervigilant, but I thought I heard the sound of someone else walking on the path. When I look around, there's not a person or animal in sight.

Animals. That's something else I never thought about. Mom was a careful person as well. Even though bears weren't typically this far south, you never knew what large animal you could find in this national park.

I shrug off my worries and continue to walk towards the water sounds until I see the river. I look around. My brother's body was found near here, I know it.

While I've only been walking for ten minutes, I imagine how difficult it would be carrying a body at night through the brush. Mickey was a slender man. I remember when I saw him two years ago for Christmas. He was so pale and skinny back then. He couldn't have weighed more than a hundred and fifty pounds soaking wet.

It was the drugs that did that to him. Before our mother passed, he looked nothing like the skeleton of the brother I met that Christmas. I imagine his appearance became even worse before his death.

While he may have been skinny and underweight, it still would have been difficult to move his body through these woods. Detective Drayson did say there was an indication that the killer used something to move his body and suggested they dragged it using a blanket.

No blanket was found near his corpse though.

Two brutes the size of Jake and Lenny could have easily brought Mickey's body through the woods. I can almost imagine the men doing it.

I stop and take a moment to myself. I wish I could disconnect my brain from thinking all the terrible thoughts and images I have right now. It's only making things worse.

I look round the forest area and the river flowing near me. I think about turning back.

What could I possibly hope to find out here? How would I even know where the police found Mickey? Unless I find a chalk outline of a dead body, finding where Mickey was discovered will be impossible.

I'm about to turn and leave when I hear movement in the trees surrounding me. I look out into the dense brush, taking a few steps backwards toward the river.

I hear steps again, and this time I know I'm not hearing things.

It's almost as if someone is following me. Watching me.

I've been feeling like this a lot lately. Sometimes I feel like someone else has been with me, even when I'm alone.

"Hello," I call out again. I listen carefully and hear more steps coming from the forest.

My eyes widen when I catch a glimpse of someone walking between the large trees. A man in a blue jacket.

CHAPTER 29

Brother

Sarah covers her mouth, attempting to prevent herself from screaming, as a stranger hides in the woods nearby.

"Who's there!" I shout as if somehow this person will hear.

Unlike before, there's no wall preventing me from figuring it out for myself. If my theory is right, I should be able to see who the stranger is so long as Sarah's nearby.

The footsteps of the man continue across the forested area, only now it sounds like he's walking past us. I still venture through the woods myself to see.

A glimpse of his blue jacket catches my attention. If I was able to breathe, this would be where I realize I'd been holding it.

When I finally see the stranger's face, my anxiety vanishes nearly instantly.

An older man, who seems to be close to seventy but in surprisingly good shape, is walking through the forest with headphones on. By his side is a small, white, fluffy dog. I'm not sure what breed it is, but for a tiny pup, it's not a loud one.

The small dog stops and stares directly at me. It

lets out a shy yelp as the man takes off his headphones. "Peaches, let's go."

The dog gives a polite bark as it looks at me, taking small-pawed steps towards me.

I smile, thinking this dog must sense me. "Peaches," I say to her. "Who's a good girl?" The dog's tail starts to wag furiously.

"What are you barking at, girl?" the old man in the blue jacket says, confused. Suddenly Sarah comes through the bushes and his eyes widen. He covers his chest.

"Are you okay?" Sarah asks.

The old man nods. "You nearly scared me to death."

"I'm so sorry," she says. "You sort of scared me, too. I thought I was by myself out here."

The old man laughs. "Well, these woods can make you feel that way. I'll be on my way, Ms." He tips an imaginary hat to Sarah before attempting to leave, but Peaches still won't budge. Instead, she continues to look directly at me, letting out another bark as her tail wags.

Sarah looks in the direction the dog is staring. Her eyes go past me.

"Bye, Peaches," I say, waving to the pile of white fluff as the old man tugs to get her to move. She finally does.

I stand beside Sarah as we watch the old man and his small dog walk through the forest. As we see him disappear into the brush, it dawns on me that the detective told my sister that it was a hiker who found my body. I even believe the officer said the man had a dog as well.

Could that have been him?

I wonder what other things this man has encountered deep in these woods. He's already discovered my body, ghouls like myself, and, well, my sister nearly scaring him to death.

Sarah takes a moment before continuing her hike.

"I wish I could help, sis," I tell her. "I don't know where I was found. What are you going to find that the police haven't even if you do discover the spot?"

She doesn't answer me and instead continues walking along the river, following the track she took to get here. She manages to eventually find the main trail, and I'm relieved that she seems to have given up looking.

Once we're back at her rental car, instead of getting inside, she leans against the vehicle, looking out into the forest.

"It is beautiful," I tell her as I do the same. "I remember all the trips here with Mom." I laugh. "When I fooled around with your friend, Bethany Coleman, I took her to the falls too. I suppose it's better you don't find that out."

I laugh again, but my sister is looking down at her feet.

Maybe she did hear me.

"What are you looking at?" I ask. Sarah continues to stare at the ground. It takes me a moment to see it for myself. Among the litter in the parking lot and cigarette butts is a tag. On it is a symbol we both recognize.

John's Hardware Store.

CHAPTER 30

Sister

I may have given up trying to find where my brother's body was found, but I haven't given up trying to find who killed him.

The tag I found in the parking lot I feel could be something. It could also be nothing at all. As Detective Drayson would tell me, I should lower my expectations.

Not everything is a clue.

For a moment, I think about calling him to share what I found but realize that would be beyond unreasonable. Calling a cop because I found garbage seems like a way of pestering someone I need on my side.

What are the chances of finding a tag belonging to my stepfather's business near where my brother's body was found?

Pinewood Springs is a small town. John's Hardware Store isn't exactly a mega chain, but many people go there.

I don't even know what product the tag is for. It could be anything. I think of what Detective Drayson shared with me. The killer attempted to dig a hole for Mickey but gave up.

My mind runs with ideas of what the tag was for, and

there's only one way to find out.

It's been years since I've been to John's store. As I pull into the parking lot, I smile at his signage. In large letters it says, "John's Hardware Store". Cartoon images of hammers and nails surround it.

It's not a very creative name, but that's John for you.

While I sit in my car, I think of the old hiker. While being terrified for my life, I forgot what Detective Drayson had said to me. My brother's body was found by a hiker... who owned a dog. I'm so stupid. That must have been the person who found Mickey.

I wonder what the chances are if I go back to the trail that I'd find him still wandering around. I can't exactly yell out the name of someone I don't know.

I could yell out his dog's name. Peaches.

There was no other car in the lot besides mine at the park. Whoever the old hiker is, he must live close by or park somewhere else. The lot I was at is the only one near the trail that goes along the river though.

I feel like I'd be wasting my time trying to find a mysterious hiker and his fluffy white dog.

As I enter my stepfather's hardware store, I continue to think about what I should do about the hiker. I know I can't ask the detective for information about him. The officer made it clear he doesn't want me involving myself any further.

As I pass the entrance, a large cutout sign of John is by the front. He's holding a hammer at his side. His other hand is by his waist. "Nobody can beat our prices," a text box says beside his head.

I remember how funny I thought it was the first time I saw it in his store. Mom took the picture of him against one of our white walls at home. Somehow he turned it into the cardboard cutout that I see in the store.

I walk up to the cashier. It's a young woman I don't recognize.

"Hi," I say with a smile. "I'm looking for John. I'm his stepdaughter."

She smiles back. "Oh, you're Sarah, right? He's mentioned you."

I'm surprised by the comment. John mentioned me to his teenaged cashier as well. How often does he talk about me?

"That's me," I say. "Is he around?"

She nods behind me. "He's out back in the delivery area. He should be out there in the yard somewhere."

I thank her as I leave the store through the back door. Through the building materials, I see John, only he's not alone. My eyes widen as I realize who he's speaking with.

I'm too far away to understand what he's saying but not far enough to not see who it is. Jake leans against his truck, speaking to John, while Lenny smokes.

I watch them from behind the stack of wood and materials as the three of them talk. John nods at Jake and takes out his wallet, handing him a stack of cash. He shakes both of their hands before Mickey's friends pile into the truck.

John watches them as they exit the back of the parking lot.

I want to leave after seeing my stepfather with them. Hadn't he said he didn't know them very well? Now he's paying them cash.

Why?

I look at the door I came out of, thinking I should just leave, but it's hard. I'm dumbfounded by what I just witnessed.

What's happening here? Why did John tell me he didn't know Jake and Lenny, but now they seem to be, what, employees? That appeared to be a large payout, and it was all in cash. I don't remember when I had a summer job with John being paid in bills.

I used to be a cashier for a few months in the summer of grade ten. Just like the young woman at the register now. When I worked for my stepfather, he paid me with a cheque.

John comes around the materials and spots me. "Hey, Sarah," he says with a smile. He looks back towards the parking lot and back at me. "Didn't think I'd see you here."

"Hey, John. I was hoping to talk to you."

"Sure, sure," he says with a friendly smile. "Let's talk in my office."

CHAPTER 31

Brother

I follow Sarah into John's office. Once inside he sits behind his desk and gestures to Sarah to take a seat.

As they greet each other, I look around the office. It all seems just as dated as John's personality.

On a corkboard near his desk, amongst the old flyers and paperwork tacked on, I spot an old photo of Mom, John and a teenaged Sarah and me. Sarah has this beaming smile, showcasing her braces. She hated them so much, but I think everyone around her had it worse. Whenever she talked, chunks of food would always somehow fling out of her mouth.

It was truly disgusting. I made fun of her that whole six months she had them, making it even worse for my sister. She got back at me, though, when the following year it was my turn to have braces.

"I don't suppose you came for our discounted hammers today?" John says with a smile.

Sarah gives a thin smile back. "That was Mickey's friends I saw with you, right?" She asks the question, but I know she already knows the answer.

She just wants to see John's reaction, I realize.

"Yeah," he answers. "Lenny and Jake."

Sarah takes a deep breath. "I'm confused. You told me you didn't know them."

"Well," John says, "I don't know them well, is what I said. They do deliveries for me sometimes. Cheap labor. They seem to like the workout." He puts up a finger. "Plus, they prefer to be paid in cash. Nice." When Sarah doesn't respond, he looks at her. "Mickey used to do deliveries with them sometimes too."

I shake my head. "Once," I say, but nobody pays attention, "I brought Jake and Lenny to the store with me once and John put us all to work. I didn't know you still had them working for you."

"I used to do it all by myself," John says, "but my back isn't the same these days." He lets out a laugh. "How have you been keeping busy?"

"I went for a hike around the national park," she says.

John raises an eyebrow. "Really." He lowers his head. "Sarah, why did you do that?"

She lets out a deep breath. "I needed to go there myself."

"Why, though?" John asks. "It's only going to make it worse for you. What are you hoping to find?"

Sarah shrugs. "I'm not sure, but I did find this in the parking lot there." She extends her hand with the tag in it.

John puts on his reading glasses. "One of mine?"

"That's right," she says. "It's probably nothing, I know, but since I found it in the parking lot, I thought it would be a good idea to check with you what this was for."

John looks at her, confused. "Why?"

She tilts her head. "I found it in the lot where Mickey's killer was. We still don't know what was used to kill him. It could be anything in this store for all we know. Or maybe it's for something else his killer used."

John stares at her a moment before nodding. "Well, I'm not sure how I can help you with this. It could be for anything."

"You could just scan it. It has a barcode on it. Your system should know."

John purses his lips, and suddenly, a smile spreads across his face. "Of course. We'll scan it." He stands up from his desk and waves for her to follow. "Back when I opened this store I used to only have paper receipts. Paper records. Everything was on paper. Times are changing, I guess." He laughs.

John walks up to the cashier. "Hey, Tina," he says to her. "Can you do me a favor and scan this barcode? I want to check what it's for."

"Sure," she says, chewing on her gum. She points her scanner at the sticker and reads the screen. "Looks like it's for a shovel."

I look at my sister in shock. Sarah's eyes haven't left our stepfather.

I watch as Sarah makes up a reason to leave suddenly. "Sorry," she says. "Drew just texted and I have to meet up with him again."

John smiles. "That's great. You guys are really starting to jump back in where you left off."

"Yeah," Sarah says nervously. "See you later."

I follow Sarah as she leaves John's Hardware Store. When she does, she stops in her tracks. Her eyes look out into the parking lot.

Initially, I wonder why she seems like she saw a ghost. Then I see them. Jake and Lenny are inside their truck, parked beside Sarah's rental.

Jake smiles at her before driving away.

CHAPTER 32

Sister

I stab the food on my plate, not really eating it but more shoving it from one side to another. I'm not hungry. I can't think straight. Ever since seeing Jake and Lenny at John's Hardware Store, my mind has been racing.

Finding out the tag was for a shovel makes me think too. Was that the shovel used to try and bury Mickey?

What are the chances a tag for a shovel would be in the parking lot of an area a killer brought a body? Although that's not confirmed. It's my own line of thought.

I need to remind myself that I'm not a detective. I have no clue what I'm doing.

I then remind myself where I am and look up at my date, who's trying his best to ensure I'm having fun.

"I'm sorry, Drew," I say to him.

He waves me off, taking a bite from his steak. "Please don't feel that way. You're going through a lot. It's okay. It was silly for me to try going on a date with you right now."

I take in a deep breath. He's probably right. I buried my brother a few days ago and now I'm on a date. A date with the same mortician who processed my brother's body. Is that what they even call it? The whole thing is morbid.

Despite that, I still wanted to see Drew tonight. I thought going out with him would help ground me back in reality.

It hasn't. All I can think about is how the day has gone. From the old hiker and his small dog to Jake and Lenny waiting for me to come back to my rental car, taunting me before they leave.

I sigh. "I'm a terrible date."

He shakes his head. "Not what I remember." He smiles at me. For a change I give him a genuine one back.

I think the idea of going out with Drew tonight was better than the reality. Drew went out of his way to pick me up at John's house as well. I almost felt like a teenager again when Alice knocked on my bedroom door to tell me Drew was waiting for me.

Thankfully, John hadn't returned home. I'm not sure I can be around him right now. I have too many questions.

I can't believe what I'm thinking about. Was the shovel used to bury my brother bought from John's store? What if it wasn't bought? What if someone took it and used it?

What if John used one of his own shovels to... I try not to think of the idea.

My mind is playing terrible tricks on me still. I keep seeing images of the old man in the blue jacket and his dog, Peaches, finding my brother's body by the river.

I hate thinking of what the killer did to my brother.

I push some mash potatoes around with my fork. When I look over at Drew's plate, I realize that he's nearly finished.

"I still can't believe you're a mortician," I say to him,

trying to find a way to get my mind off my brother's death. When I realize I'm talking to a mortician, I know I'm failing.

Drew smiles. "I know." He lets out a heavy breath. "It's a hard job sometimes. A lot of emotions around me all day. It's been a few years since I started work, but I'm still not used to it. When I first got my summer job at the cemetery, I thought it would just be for the season. The owner offered me an apprenticeship, though. A few years later, and I'm a certified mortician."

"Certified. I didn't know there was such a registry for your kind," I say to him playfully. My banter stops when I think of Mickey again. "Do you like your job?"

He nods. "I do, actually. As strange as that may seem."

"You're around death... all day. I have a hard time understanding how you could."

He gives a thin smile. "I like to think I'm helping people. Helping the family and loved ones of the deceased by giving them the best support I can during one of their hardest days of their life."

I nod and glance down at my cold mashed potatoes and uneaten steak. "That makes sense." I look up at Drew, trying my best to not cry in front of him. "What do you think happens after someone... you know?"

"Passes?" he asks. "I'm not sure. I like to think something happens though. The idea that we wouldn't exist is too scary. I like to think I'll see my loved ones who have passed when I join them."

I give a wry smile. "So you believe in spirits?"

He sighs. "Not like ghosts or anything scary, but I do think our loved ones can be with us even after they've passed." I lower my head. "Are you okay, Sarah?" he asks me. He puts down his knife and fork. "I'll get the bill and take you home. I'm sorry."

"No, I'm okay," I tell him. "I guess the reason I ask is because ever since I've come back to Pinewood Springs, I feel like he's around me. Mickey. I feel his presence. It's strange, but even now I feel like he's here, with me." I look at Drew, who's smiling at me. "Okay, I know I'm coming off like I'm crazy. I probably feel this way because I'm back in town, and having these constant attacks of nostalgia from when I was younger. I'm sure these feelings are normal and part of the grieving process... or whatever."

"Maybe," Drew says, taking a sip of his wine. "I don't think you're crazy, though." He looks around and leans in closer to me. "I'll tell you something I haven't told anyone before. Do you remember how I talked about my grandma?"

I let out a laugh. "Yes. Grandma Sherry, right?"

He nods. "Well, she meant a lot to me as a kid. As you may remember, I was only like eight when she passed. I was heartbroken. It was my first funeral. The first time someone I loved passed. I spent most Fridays with my grandma. Mom would pick me up the next day. Grandma and I would cook together, watch television, play board games. I loved just talking to her." Drew smiles. "She would hum this old timey song while I played with my toys or while she was cooking. I don't even know what the song was, but I wish I could find out. Her voice always comforted me." He lowers his head. "When I was at her funeral, I couldn't understand that the same woman who I loved, who tucked me in every Friday, was gone. Soon after she passed, though, I felt like she was near me. I'm not sure what it was. When I had sad thoughts about my grandma, it was as if she was there, wiping my tears away, comforting me."

I reach out across the table. "I don't think that's crazy at all. I feel the same way."

"I haven't gotten to the strange part yet," he says, looking at me, gripping my hand. "Sometimes, when I was in my room, alone, playing with my toys, I felt I could hear her humming her song." Drew quickly wipes his eyes.

"You heard her humming her song?" I ask.

He nods. "I swear, I did. And maybe you think that sounds scary, because reflecting on it now, it kind of sounds spooky." He straightens up in his chair. "It wasn't, though. Grandma stayed behind to help me get through her death. Help me come to terms with it. It was only for a short period of time that I felt her presence. It was as if my grandmother could feel my love for her, even after she passed, and she was drawn to it. My love for her kept her with me until I was ready to let go."

"You never told me that story before," I say, surprised.

He lets out a laugh. "You can see why. I must seem like the crazy one now."

I grip his hand tighter. "We can be crazy together," I say.

He smiles at me, and when he does, it's as if I see the boy who I fell in love with all those years ago in school. I also see the boy who dumped me. Left me wondering what I had done for him to leave me so abruptly.

I let go of his hand. "I have to ask. Why did you break things off with me so suddenly?"

He purses his lips. "I was wondering when you'd ask. I thought about bringing it up myself."

"Was it something I had done?"

He shakes his head. "No, not exactly. Those times were tough for you. With your mother sick, and you wanting to go to university, I knew you wanted to leave this town. I understood why. I didn't want to leave town, though. I felt my place was still here. I knew yours was somewhere else. I was worried that if we continued to be together, you wouldn't have left. I would have been a reason you stayed. I couldn't bear the idea."

I lower my head. "We could have made it work," I say. "You didn't trust me in a long-distance relationship?"

"No," he says quickly. "Not at all. I always trusted you. I just felt you'd outgrown this town. You'd outgrown me."

I shake my head. "Well, I guess you really are crazy." I pick up my wine glass and take a sip as he does as well. We smile as our eyes meet.

CHAPTER 33

Brother

I sit between my sister and her ex-boyfriend as they continue with their "date". At first there was quite a bit of tension from my sister. As the conversation lightened, though, and they talked more and more about old times, the more flirtatious side of both of them showed.

Unfortunately for me.

This has to be the most uncomfortable I've ever been in my life, and I'm dead.

As their conversation became more sexually tense instead of reminiscent, I looked for ways out. When I attempted to escape the restaurant, whatever force keeps me here won't let me leave my sister's sight.

It's almost like we're tied at the hip, like we're sharing the same womb again.

There are differences, though. When she's sleeping, or in the bathroom, somehow the connection fades temporarily. I'm not completely metaphysically tied to my sister, but for whatever reason, I'm stuck here.

As Sarah finally manages to finish her steak, I'm hopeful that we'll be leaving soon. That's not the case either. Of course the two order a dessert. Just one. They share it.

How cute. How adorable. *Please save me.*

The two banter back and forth as I watch, my cries for the date to end going unnoticed.

When the dessert is finished and their drinks drunk, the couple stare at each other awkwardly in silence. I can feel the tension continue to escalate. It's like watching a bad romance movie but not being able to change the channel... or switch off the television.

I turn to my sister and sigh. "I'm glad my death has somehow brought you back to the mortician, but I'm ready to leave now. How about you?"

Drew beats me to it. "Well, thanks for letting me take you out for dinner. I had fun catching up."

"Me too," Sarah says with a thin smile. "I needed this, so I should be thanking you."

Drew looks innocently around the room and back into my sister's eyes. "I'm wondering, though, if maybe you'd like to come over for coffee?"

"Coffee?" my sister repeats.

Drew smiles. "Yeah. Catch up some more."

I can almost see my sister turn red. She's about to melt in her seat.

"Coffee?" I scoff. "Drew, I have to give it to you, man. A well-played move here, but I think it's getting late, and we should—"

"I'd love to," my sister interrupts. I feel utterly defeated.

I reluctantly follow them to Drew's car. I make a crack about how he should have picked up Sarah in his hearse, but neither of them finds me funny. They're too busy flirting with each other.

Drew opens the passenger door for Sarah as she climbs inside. This time I don't join them.

"Hey," I say to Drew as he circles around his car, "you two have fun." I point a finger at him playfully. "And have her back before midnight. Don't do anything I wouldn't do." I realize what I'm saying. "Wait, don't do what I'd do. Don't have too much fun, you kids."

Drew steps inside the car and turns on the ignition. I smile to myself as he backs out of his parking spot slowly. "Well, goodnight," I say, amazed.

I wasn't able to leave rooms unless my sister was near me, but now she's going with Drew. My smile widens as I watch them leave the parking lot.

As they drive down the street, I laugh to myself. I was scared to death, poor phrasing in my case, but very concerned that I'd have to go with Sarah to Drew's house for them to have "coffee".

Knowing how boring my sister is, there is still a solid chance that's all that would have happened. Thankfully, I won't have to find out.

I laugh again as I watch Drew's car turn down a street and go completely out of sight. I look around the parking lot of the steakhouse, not knowing what I should do with my time now.

As I think about it, I blink and suddenly I'm in the back seat of Drew's car listening to him and Sarah's flirtatious talk.

"What the he—" I lean back in the chair. "I give up."

Being dead sucks.

CHAPTER 34
Sister

Drew leans his body against mine, our lips continuing to battle each other for dominance. Every so often I feel I'm winning until Drew picks up again and I succumb to his will. Our mouths haven't left each other's since we entered his house.

It's animalistic.

It's as if we're making up for the years we've been apart in the last twenty minutes. Despite how good his lips feel on mine, and the tingling across my skin, I'm also battling an upset stomach.

Maybe it was the steak. As Drew introduces his tongue, my thoughts go right back to him.

For a moment, his lips detach from mine, and he takes a long breath. "I didn't think that would happen," he says with a thin smile. "I actually did just want coffee with you."

I laugh. "We'll still have a cup." I was worried that as our kisses became more sensual that he'd start becoming more adventurous, but his hands have been just as polite as he is. The perfect gentleman.

And that's good. I don't want to take things too far. I was worried that by accepting his invitation to come over he'd take it that I'd want to jump right into bed, but that's not the case.

I'm okay with just his lips on mine. It's innocent and feels nice. Takes me back in time to when life made more sense. When my mom was alive and so was Mickey. When I wasn't trying to figure out who murdered my sibling.

I try not to think about it as he stares intimately into my eyes. "I can take that coffee now," I tell him.

He pats my upper thigh as he gets up from the couch. "You still take it with two sugars and a little cream?"

I smile and nod back. "I do, actually."

"Be right back," he says as he walks into his kitchen and out of sight. "My mom bought me one of those fancy coffee makers last Christmas," he yells. "I don't use it nearly as much as I should."

"How is your mom?" I ask, curious.

"Doing well," he shouts back. I can hear him turn on the coffee maker and open the fridge. As the machine grumbles and starts pouring coffee, I take off my jean jacket.

I barely had time to settle into Drew's place before we were all over each other. I'm pretty sure I was the one who initiated the kissing. I didn't realize it would turn into a half-hour marathon. Time felt frozen as we kissed but it actually flew by.

I smile as I think of it and hope he comes back soon.

He keeps a tidy home. Clean and nicely decorated. I'm not sure what to expect from a mortician. Taxidermy animals maybe, or something weird like that. But it's all normal, and thankfully, so is Drew.

When I spot his closet by the door, I walk up to it. When I open the door I grab a hanger and put my jacket on the rack.

Before I close the door, something on the shelf above the rack catches my attention. A lamp with vines and flowers painted on it. The same one that was missing from Mickey's living room. The same lamp I believe was used to kill my brother.

Drew walks into the living room with two mugs in his hands. His smile drops when he sees me by the closet.

"What are you doing?" he asks.

I stand on my tippy toes and grab the lamp, feeling its weight in my hands before showing him.

He looks nearly as surprised as I do. "I found one on Facebook Marketplace. I was surprised too. I grabbed it after work."

I feel the cast iron lamp in my hand. It's certainly heavy enough to hurt someone, especially if it was used forty-one times.

"You just have it in your closet?" I ask, confused, my face giving away my disgust. "Why didn't you say something before?"

Drew takes a deep breath. "I was going to mention it, but I wanted us to just have fun today. I didn't want to talk about it right away. I thought maybe later or a different day."

I scoff. As I examine it, it does seem to be newer than the one Mom bought so many years ago. When I look at Drew, though, he has this face like I caught him stealing.

Suddenly the idea of kissing him repulses me.

"I... think I'm going to leave," I say, putting it back on the shelf.

"Wait," Drew says, taking a step forward.

I put my hand up. "No, that's okay. I'd rather just go." I grab my jean jacket and put it on quickly.

He quickly puts the cups down on the living room

table. "Well, let me drive you at least."

I shake my head. I remember I saw a convenience store nearby as Drew drove us here. "That's okay. I'll get a taxi."

"A taxi?" Drew repeats. "Why? Because you found the lamp in my closet? You asked me to look into it for you, and I did. I actually went out and found one. I figured you'd be happy."

I look at him, and as innocent as he seems, I can't think straight. After my talks with Mickey's girlfriend, seeing Jake and Lenny talking to John, I'm not sure what to believe or who to trust.

"Thanks for taking me out," I say to Drew as I open his front door. "I had fun. I did."

It's true. A part of me knows I'm overreacting. Or maybe my body is trying to tell me something.

The police say that it may have been an act of violence committed against my brother. A robbery gone wrong. Someone from his world of crime that killed him.

What if the police are wrong?

What if I've been staying in the killer's house? What if I was just kissing my brother's murderer?

"You don't trust me?" Drew says, confused.

I'm about to close his door and leave, but an image of Lenny and Jake waiting for me outside my stepfather's hardware store hits me. I look down the empty streets for any oncoming vehicles or parked ones. When I don't see any red trucks, I look back at Drew.

I take a deep breath. "I'm not sure I can trust anyone right now."

CHAPTER 35

Brother

I was thankful that the date was over, but as I watch my sister turn into a ball of anxiety, I can't help but feel terrible. Nearly as terrible as I felt watching them make out. If I wasn't already dead, I'd wish death upon me for being stuck in that room.

I understand my sister's fears though. Seeing the lamp in Drew's house freaked her out. Seeing John speak to Jake and Lenny scared her. She's starting to suspect that someone is lying.

And she should.

I'm scared for my sister, but I've given up trying to tell her what to do. I've wanted her to leave town since the day of my funeral. I mean, going to the bar and talking to people like Jake Matthews and Lenny Mercer will only bring trouble into your life, or worse.

Not enough attention is being given to my ex-girlfriend. I broke up with her and soon after, I'm dead.

It feels like everyone is lying. I'm surprised Sarah wants to come back to John's house given what she must be thinking right now.

When the taxi pulls up, she slowly gets out and walks up the steps. I reluctantly follow her.

All the lights are on inside, and my sister takes a moment to look in the windows. She takes a deep breath while I stand beside her.

"What are we doing coming back here?" I ask. "Why are you still here? You're scared. I know you are. Let's just go. I give you permission to leave town. Do not feel obligated to stay here because of me."

Alice opens the door and gives Sarah a surprised look. "Did you forget your key?" she asks.

Sarah shakes her head. "I was looking for it in my purse," she lies.

She hadn't even put her hand in her purse. I can tell she was scared to go inside. After she freaked out on Drew, she doesn't know who she can trust or what to believe.

"Did you come home in a taxi?" Alice asks. She looks at Sarah's somber expression. "Sorry, look at me being all nosey. Come inside." She steps away for Sarah to enter.

"Sister!" Melanie calls out to her from her playroom as she scribbles on her page.

Sarah manages a thin smile back. "Good evening, sister," she says back.

I grin as well. At least we can trust Melanie.

Sarah looks around. "John not here?" she asks.

Alice shakes her head. "Still at the shop working late."

"Working?" I say, surprised. I look over at a clock on a side table. It's nearly nine at night. I remember how my mom hated it when John would work late, but he would never be out past dark.

"I was just about to get Melanie to bed," Alice says. "Say goodnight to Sarah," she says, looking at her daughter.

"Goodnight, sister," Melanie says through grinning teeth.

Sarah laughs. I can't help but do the same. Melanie's expression and happiness always filled my heart, even for someone like me who would always be beating myself up for whatever I'd injected or put in my mouth. Melanie was a reminder of the good in the world.

Sarah wishes her goodnight as well before going upstairs to her room. When she steps inside, she shuts the door behind her. I expect her to take out her laptop and continue to pretend to be a detective. For once, though, she surprises me.

She opens the closet and takes out her suitcase. She opens it on the bed and starts filling it with her clothes.

"Finally," I say to her. I wish I could help her pack.

The sound of smashed glass makes her jump. Melanie screams downstairs. Her shriek grows when a second window breaks.

It's coming from downstairs.

Sarah opens her bedroom door. She sees Alice holding Melanie tightly, coming up the stairs. Melanie's covering her ears and rocking herself rhythmically back and forth.

"Is she hurt?" Sarah asks.

"We're fine," Alice says. "Just scared. It came from the living room."

Without hesitation, Sarah quickly gets to the ground floor. Scared myself, I try to run in front of my sister as if to protect her from whatever happened.

When we get to the living room, we confirm both the large windows in the front of the house have been bashed in. Broken glass is scattered over the entire room.

As I can no longer feel pain, I run across the floor and

look outside. No one is there.

A large rock with red paint is lying near Sarah's feet. She picks it up and her eyes widen. Her hand lowers to the floor, and the rock slips from her grip.

From across the room, I realize that the red paint on the rock says something. A word. I tilt my head to read better. I'm frozen in fear as I let it sink in. In bold red letters, it says: "LEAVE."

CHAPTER 36
Sister

I called the police and Alice called John. It was John who arrived first.

When the police came, the two officers spoke to each of us separately. John joked to one of the officers that thankfully he owned a hardware store and could get cheap replacement windows.

The officer smiled but I didn't find it funny. It was as if he was making light of a scary situation. It was not like John. That was Mickey's role in the family.

As the officers left, Alice sat with Melanie in her arts room. The young girl was still shaking and nervous. Despite small pieces of glass in the living room, Melanie insisted on going to her crafts room to draw. It was the only thing that calmed her. Alice allowed it but she had to wait for John to sweep and vacuum what he could in the living room first.

It was nearly eleven at night and way past the girl's bedtime, but she would not be going to sleep anytime soon.

When she settled, John came up the stairs and knocked on the bedroom door. When I opened it, he noticed the suitcase on the bed.

"What did Alice say to you?" he asks.

"Nothing," I say, folding some more clothes into it.

"She asked you to leave?"

I shake my head. "No, but after what happened, I should."

He nods. "That's probably not a bad idea. It's scary what happened. So, you really didn't see who it was?"

I shake my head again. "No. I was upstairs." I take a deep breath. "Maybe it was your *helpers*, Jake and Lenny."

"My helpers?" he repeats, confused. "I told you before, I don't really know them. You think it was them who broke the window?"

"I don't know," I say. "I do know someone is trying to scare me into leaving town, and it's working." Our eyes meet a moment before he looks away.

"I can take care of your rental," he says. "Don't worry about it. I can drive you to the airport for the next flight. Did you look up departures?"

"I'm not leaving town," I say confidently. "I'm just not staying here. Whatever is happening, I don't want your family impacted." I peer at his eyes as I say the words to see how he responds.

"You're not leaving town?" he says, confused. I nod. "Sarah, I say this out of concern for your wellbeing: I think after what happened tonight, it's better if you go back to Toronto."

"Really? A broken window or two isn't a big deal for you. You own a hardware store."

He laughs, but when I don't reciprocate, he looks at me strangely. "What are you saying?"

"I'm not sure about anything I say or what other people do." I shut my case and zip it closed. "All I know is my brother is dead, and I'm the only one who seems to care about figuring out who did it!"

"That's not fair," he says. "I care. I care a lot."

I leave the room without saying a word and storm down the stairs. Alice looks surprised as I walk by with the suitcase. Melanie loses her calm demeanor and suddenly looks scared.

"Sister, leave?" she asks.

I take a deep breath. "Yes, sweetie. I'm leaving."

"Come back soon?" she asks.

I shake my head. "Sorry, but I don't think so."

Alice stands beside her daughter. "We talked about this, Melanie. Sarah wasn't staying for a long time. She was going to leave sooner or later."

Melanie looks at me and back at her mom. "Cause sister sad?"

Alice takes a moment before answering. "Sarah is sad, yes."

"For brother?" Melanie says, confused again.

Alice breathes out. "Yes, Melanie."

Melanie looks around the room. She points at one of her pictures she made with her in the car with other stick figures. "Mickey. Back! Sleeping."

Alice tilts her head. "Yes, sleeping, but Sarah is still sad."

I shake my head. "No! Stop telling her things like that, Alice. Mickey is not sleeping. Mickey is not coming back. Our brother is gone, Melanie. He's dead. Don't you understand? He's in heaven. He will never come back!"

Melanie's eyes start to water. Alice quickly wraps her arm around her daughter, trying her best to conceal her whimpers.

I take a step towards them. "I'm so sorry, Alice. Melanie, I didn't mean to come off so—"

"Maybe it is time to leave, Sarah," Alice tells me.

CHAPTER 37

Brother

This is beyond dumb, and all I can do is watch it happen.

I follow my sister as she checks into a motel right outside of town by the highway. Everything about it seems like it came right out of the movie *Psycho*.

It looks like the perfect place to be murdered in, but for some reason, my dear sister seems content to stay here for the night or longer.

As she steps into her room, she turns on the lights. I may be dead but even I can smell the musty odour the room offers.

Again, the ideal place to stay, especially after what happened at John's house.

I shake my head as I follow my sister inside. "You should have taken John's offer and let him drive you to the airport. You should have let him take your rental back, or drive it yourself to the airport. What are you trying to prove here, Sarah? Let the police do their job."

Sarah walks through me and out the door, and for a moment, I wonder if she's found some sense, but instead she comes back, rolling her luggage behind her.

She puts it beside the bed and closes the front door.

Before she locks it, she looks outside through the large front window.

"Even if there was someone out there, you wouldn't care," I scoff and lower my head, trying to explain my worries. "I'm scared. I'm scared for you. You really think this will end with property damage? What happened at John's house is a warning."

I think of my former friends, Jake and Lenny. I never took them to be so subtle in their approach to scaring someone. Usually they'd burst through the door, break your legs and leave.

What if they weren't the ones who threw the rocks? What if it was someone else?

As my sister gets ready to sleep, I sit on her bed trying to piece it all together. None of it makes sense. It feels like Sarah's uncovered so much in the past few days. The letter at my grave, finding that the house key in the fake rock is missing, the lamp is gone from the living room, the missing picture of me and Jenn. It feels like all of these things could be important in solving what happened to me. It also could be a bunch of nothing.

The letter by my grave was from my father. That clue turned out to be nothing.

It feels like we're so close to figuring this out. My sister slips into the bed and turns her head away from me. A large beam of light shines through the edges of the blackout curtains. It's so bright that even Sarah opens her eyes and looks at the window.

"I know this is a bad time to say I told you so, so I won't," I say to her.

The lights turn off, but now I hear voices coming from outside the door. Suddenly the handle turns, but thankfully Sarah had locked it.

My eyes are just as wide eyed as Sarah's as I watch in fear.

"Who's there?" she shouts from her bed. "I'm calling the police!"

"Just call them already!" I yell at her.

Instead, Sarah gets out of the bed and peeps through the hole. She takes a step back and looks confused.

"Who's there?" I ask her. Sarah unlocks the door and begins to open it. "What are you doing?" I yell. "Don't go out there. Haven't you seen scary movies before? Never leave the room!"

She doesn't listen. I quickly follow her. We're equally surprised when we see a young man and woman using their key to open the door to the room beside us.

"So sorry! Wrong room," the woman says with an awkward smile.

"We didn't mean to scare you," the man adds.

Sarah smiles back. "No problem. Have a good night."

"You as well!" the woman says. They enter their room and close the door.

When Sarah goes back into her room, she shuts and locks the door behind her.

"Tomorrow, we leave, okay?" I say to her. "Please."

Sarah gets back into bed and closes her eyes. As she drifts to sleep, I disappear.

CHAPTER 38

Brother

Sarah's eyes open quickly to the sound of a car alarm going off.

I quickly notice it's daytime. Sarah runs to the curtains and looks through. Her mouth gapes open as she opens the door.

"What now?" I say as I see for myself.

The rental car is destroyed. The windshield is smashed, the back window broken, a front tire slashed, and a large scratch mark runs across one side of the car.

The man from the room next door steps out, rubbing his eyes. "Can you please turn off your alarm? It's—" His eyes widen as he sees what happened. He quickly runs to his jeep parked nearby and you can almost see the worry melt as he realizes his vehicle is unharmed.

Sarah goes back inside, grabs the car keys and turns off the alarm.

She looks inside her rental. Broken glass covers the backseat from the smashed window. Shards of glass cover the driver's seat. She traces her hand across the large scratch on the car, shaking her head.

"I told you so!" I shout. "I'll be that guy, I don't care. I. Told. You. So."

Sarah covers her eyes in disbelief.

I quickly look around. Whoever did this to her car could still be nearby. All I see is a van driving down the highway.

I look in the motel parking lot, hoping to see someone in one of the cars. No one else is in the parking lot though. No red truck. No Lenny or Jake.

If this was them, they were smart enough to have one of them be a getaway driver.

"Did you see who did this?" the man from next door asks my sister. Sarah doesn't respond and instead covers her mouth, looking at the destruction.

"And," I shout at her, "who told you to get rental insurance when you got the car? Me! You never listen to anyone."

"Was that, like, an ex-boyfriend?" the woman from next door says, stepping out of the room and looking at the car.

"No," Sarah says quietly.

I see someone from a few doors down looking through their curtains at us. We're starting to get attention now. Sarah takes out her phone.

"Good call," I say. "Call the police. Call that detective guy."

"Hey," she says in a voice that tells me she's not calling the cops. "It's Sarah. I was hoping you could help me today with something for a few hours. I know it's last minute, but it's urgent." She pauses a moment. "Thanks, Drew."

"Your boyfriend?" I say amused. "You called your ex-boyfriend? The one you ran out on the other night? You're too much, sis."

I wait with her until he arrives, complaining to her

the entire time about how dumb she's acting. My sister, being the most stubborn woman I know, surprisingly doesn't listen.

Drew pulls into the lot and parks across from the wreck of the rental. He takes off his sunglasses to see the damage for himself.

"Are you okay?" he asks Sarah.

"No!" I answer for her. "She's not! She's too stupid to see how much danger she's in right now. Tell her, Drew. Talk her out of being stupid."

"I know it was them," Sarah says. "They're trying to scare me. Run me out of town. I'm close. I know it."

"Who?" Drew asks.

"Those two walking meat sticks," she says as she scoffs. "They killed my brother. I know it." She looks at Drew. "And I need your help to prove it."

"Me?" he says, confused.

She nods. "I want to talk to Mickey's girlfriend again. Jenn. She knows more, and it's time she comes clean."

Drew looks at the car. "This is too much, Sarah. If you really think they killed your brother, and now they're trying to scare you, maybe you should take their warning. This could get worse."

"Yes!" I shout, raising my hands. "Finally, another person with the ability to think."

She shakes her head. "I'm so close," she says again. "I know who did this, now I just have to prove it."

Drew lowers his head. "And you believe speaking to Jenn again will help you?"

She nods. When Drew doesn't respond, Sarah takes out her phone. "Sorry. I shouldn't have called you for this. I'll take a taxi or something."

"Why did you call?" he asks.

"I need a ride," Sarah says with a smile. When he doesn't respond, my sister's smile leaves her face. For a change, she shows her fears. "I'm scared, but I can't leave town. Not yet. Not when I'm so close!"

Drew takes a moment and nods. "Fine. I'll drive."

As I watch them get into his car, I stand in disbelief, looking at her rental. "This is stupid. This is beyond stupid. You're going to get yourself killed!" I run up to her door and shout at her some more through her open window. "You say you're the only one who cares to find out who killed me, Sarah, but you don't care about what it does to you. Well, I do! I'm done with this! I'm done following you around. You're going to wind up six feet under like me, and I'm not going to watch it happen. Now, please, stop!"

Drew turns on the ignition and puts the car in reverse. Before he presses the gas, he looks at Sarah. "So, I guess this means you trust me again?"

Sarah nods. "Everybody trusts a mortician."

Drew looks at her strangely. "I don't think that's a saying, but it should be."

I shake my head. "I'm not coming. Not this time. I'd rather not exist than watch you put yourself in danger, Sarah. I'm not following you anymore. I can't do it."

If drugs were what brought me to an early grave, my sister's stubbornness will do the same. I understand why the people I love were so angry at me. They knew I was killing myself but could do nothing to save me.

As I watch Sarah leave, I get it now.

Drew backs out of his spot and exits onto the highway. I watch as they leave and pray that I won't materialize in their car again. I pray that whatever existence I have comes to an end. I wanted to watch over my sister after I passed. I wanted to be there for her. Help her grieve.

She'd rather get herself killed.

I won't be there for that.

I close my eyes and concentrate on those feelings, and as I do, my world turns black.

CHAPTER 39
Sister

Drew drives up to Jenn's address. I ask if he's okay to stay in the car while I speak with her. He agrees and I step out, walking slowly up her steps.

I don't even know what I'm going to say. I don't exactly have a plan. I do have a hunch, though. She knows more.

Her refusal to speak to the police all but confirms it. At first I thought that was because she killed Mickey herself.

After meeting Lenny and Jake and them following me in their truck, I'm realizing that may not be true.

She's involved somehow, though. The three of them could be working together in some way.

I wish I had the power to point my finger at her and magically compel her to tell the truth. Why can't life be that easy?

I'm still shaken up after finding my rental destroyed.

I bet whoever did it thought I'd run out of town. Escape back to Toronto.

They don't know me. All their scare tactic did was confirm that I'm close to the truth. My brother's killer or killers know I'm a threat. As I walk up the steps to Jenn's house, I remind myself of that.

I knock on the door. After I do, I hope her mother isn't the one to answer again. The last thing I want is to have an awkward conversation with her as well.

When I don't hear movement inside, I look at the front windows. My mouth drops open when I see one of them is broken as well and taped up with black cardboard. I was so wrapped up in my head when I came up to the house, I didn't even notice it.

Just like John's window, hers is broken.

This is certainly not a coincidence.

When I peer through the undamaged window, I see a silhouette of a slender woman peeking out from behind a wall. When my eyes meet Jenn's, she lowers her head.

"Just leave!" she shouts at me.

"I just want to talk, please," I say.

"We already did," she says. "Now go. Just go away."

I shake my head. "Just a few minutes."

"I'll call the police!"

"Good!" I shout back. "I'm not moving. Call them. I'm sure when they roll up with their sirens, you'll end up with a few more broken windows... or worse."

She doesn't respond immediately. She hides behind the wall further out of sight. I wonder if she's trying to leave through the back door. If she does, what would I even do?

Chase her?

Jenn comes out from behind the wall. She looks out onto the street around me. "Who's that?" she asks, nodding towards Drew in the car.

"He's with me," I tell her.

Jenn opens the door and tells me to get inside quickly. She turns to me, wide eyed. "You can't stay here.

You can't stay outside on my porch either."

"Or else what?" I ask. "Jake and Lenny said they'd hurt you, didn't they?"

Jenn takes a deep breath. "There's nothing we can do about it. Mickey's dead. I don't want me or you to join him."

"They came after me too," I tell her. "Jake and Lenny followed me in their truck one night. They broke a window at my stepfather's house. They destroyed my rental."

She lets out a heavy breath. "And you're still here talking to me? Believe me, these men are not to be messed with. They won't stop."

"I won't either," I tell her. "They killed Mickey, didn't they?" She doesn't answer. "Did you help them?" I cover my mouth. "Did you do something to hurt Mickey?"

She shakes her head with a look of disgust. "No! I loved him. Even when he dumped me, I couldn't let him go."

I breathe out, trying to find the words. "What happened?"

She lowers her head. "You should just leave." She looks at me, her eyes filled with fear. "They'll kill us."

"I'm not running. You shouldn't either. You loved my brother. Help me take down his killers."

She looks down again. "Even if we report them to the police, what happens next? What happens if they get to me before the police arrest them? What if they get out of jail? What if they're set free? Don't you see? It's not worth it."

"Mickey's worth it," I tell her. "His life meant something to us. He meant something to you. That's why you grabbed the photo of you two in his bedroom."

Jenn turns away with a thin smile. "We took that picture when Mickey took me on a date, downtown Calgary." She looks at me. "I'm not safe here."

"What if you weren't here?" I say. "You can come to Toronto with me. Or somewhere else. I'm selling Mickey's house. I can afford to put you up somewhere for a little bit. I'll even pay for your rehab. Mickey wrote about how you wanted to quit together."

Jenn scoffs. "You haven't thought this through. And... I've managed to stop using the past few weeks. After Mickey was killed. I was too scared to start again."

"Scared because of Jake and Lenny," I say. "Just tell me the truth. Mickey deserves that much."

Jenn lowers her head. "Okay," she says softly. She seems surprised by her own words, and so do I. Apparently I do have the power to get people to tell the truth, without magic.

She sits on the couch, covering her face. "I haven't been able to eat, sleep, or do anything since that day. I'm just so scared." Jenn looks at me, and I again reassure her she'll be okay. "The day he was killed, he broke things off with me." She lets out a nervous laugh. "It's sort of something I've grown used to. Us breaking up. It's either him or me doing it and this time it was his turn. He said he needed change. He had to stop using, or he'd die. That meant he had to stop seeing me. Stop being friends with people like Jake and Lenny." She shakes her head. "As I left his house, I was broken inside. I took a bus back to the city. Along the way, though, I had to see him again. Even though we had broken up a handful of times, something in his voice told me this time things might actually be over. I had to see him again. When I came back and knocked on his door, he didn't answer. The back door was unlocked. When I went inside, Mickey wasn't there. All I saw was the blood. It was everywhere."

I lower my head. "I saw it too." An image of a pile of dried blood in the living room and the trail of red leading to the kitchen hits me.

She takes a deep breath. "I freaked out. I thought about calling the cops but was worried I'd be arrested."

"Why?"

Jenn looks away from me. "I'm not exactly a good person. I've been in trouble before." She lowers her head. "I was scared. I called Jake and Lenny. They came by so fast. It only took them a few minutes to get there."

"Did they have blood on their shirts or anything like that?"

"No," she says. She sighs. "They told me to stand in the corner while they searched the house."

"For drugs?" I ask.

She nods. "As they searched and collected what they needed, I went up the stairs. I just wanted to get away from them. Their faces scared me. They had this intensity in their eyes. I was worried my blood would be spilt on the floor next. When I went into Mickey's room, I stayed on his bed, holding the picture frame of us." She shakes her head. "Lenny forced me out of the room. Before he did, I took the photo." She looks at me wide eyed. "I thought they might kill me there. Instead, they drove me home. They said if I spoke to the police, my body would never be found."

As Jenn's eyes start to water, I do my best to console her.

"We can't let them get away with this," I tell her. "They won't stop, and you know it. You'll be scared the rest of your life."

"I'm just so terrified. I'm so tired."

"I promise you, you'll be safe. If Mickey were here, he'd tell you what a promise from me means." I lower my head, not knowing how to convince her. "Let's do this for my brother. Mickey loved you. You loved my brother. He deserves justice. Stand up with me."

Jenn wipes her tears and tries her best to compose herself, sniffling several times.

CHAPTER 40

Sister

Drew drives us directly to the police station. I call Detective Drayson prior to us arriving. He's waiting for us when we pull up.

He interviews Jenn for over an hour. Within hours, he manages to get a judge to sign off on a warrant for Lenny Mercer and Jake Matthews.

Both men are found at Jake's house. Both men are arrested. Both men are now at the same station we are, in a holding cell.

Lenny apparently resisted his arrest, which will likely add more charges for him down the road. Jake went willingly. I always thought he seemed to be the smarter of the two meat sticks.

Detective Drayson continued speaking with Jenn while all this happens. I stay at the station the entire time, waiting for her. Drew is by my side.

As Drew and I start talking about grabbing a late lunch together, the detective comes from the back with Jenn. The two of them shake hands.

"How are you getting home, Ms. Harring?" he asks her.

I look at Drew, who nods. "We can take her," I say.

The detective smiles at me. "Good. That's probably best." He looks at me. "I wanted to give you some updates in private."

Drew smiles. "Let's wait in the car, Jenn."

Jenn gives me a thin smile. I'm not sure what she's thinking. She must be nervous. Both Jake and Lenny have been arrested and charged with my brother's murder. They're only a few meters away from us now.

"You did great," I tell her.

She nods. She and Drew leave the station. I follow the detective to his office in the back. As soon as he shuts his door, he jumps right into it. I can tell it's all good news by the smile plastered on his face.

"I just got a call from the officers at Jake Matthews' house," he says. "They found multiple bags of different kinds of illicit drugs. One of the packages had blood on it. Now, forensics will be testing it, but if the blood belongs to your brother, that's a nail in the coffin for both of them. With testimony from Ms. Harring, it looks like we have a solid case."

I let out a breath. "That's all great. What's the 'but'?"

"*But* nothing," he says with a smile. "Whenever we get the bad guys, I can't help but smile like this. If there is a but, it's a polite one. You did great. Forensics tells me after examining the information you sent on the missing lamp that it's comparable to the injuries found on your brother. We could have a match. If it wasn't for your observations and your own interrogations, I wouldn't have this wide smile plastered on my face. But... and here's the *but*... Jake Matthews and Lenny Mercer have been arrested. Now comes the gruelling process of putting together the case for trial. Unless you become a lawyer overnight, this is where you have to stop."

I nod. "I get it. I've been complicating things."

"This could have turned out different," he says. "These men are dangerous. You did great, but let us take over now. We don't want to compromise the investigation now that they're arrested."

"Understood," I say. "Can you have your men searching their houses look for any kind of shovel? I found a tag that belonged to my stepfather's hardware store in the parking lot of Pinewood Springs National Park, close to where Mickey's body was found. When I brought John the tag, he scanned it and confirmed it's for a shovel."

He purses his lips. "I'll give them a call, but this is what I mean, Sarah. Us being able to use the tag in a trial may be harder to do now. How would it look to a juror that the sister found a tag for a shovel in a lot where a body was found nearby? It complicates things. You still have the tag?"

"I do," I say. I shake my head in disbelief. "I was just trying to help."

"I know you were, but now that the men are arrested, and we already have a solid case, we don't want to complicate anything."

I take in a deep breath. "You have my word. I'm done." I think of how fearful Jenn was. "What will happen to Jake and Lenny now? Is there any way they'll be released?"

He smiles again. "Not a remote chance."

I nod. "Jenn's rightfully scared. Me too, for that matter. If they were to be released, we need to know right away."

"They won't be, but if something happens, I'll call both of you personally. And you have my word on that."

I smile. "Thanks. So, what happens from here?"

"Well, I'm about to join the officers at Jake's house, and after that I'll check in on Lenny's house. If we're lucky, we'll find the murder weapon. We'll tie up this investigation with a bow if we do. I told the officers to look out for a white cast iron lamp." He leans back in his chair. "What about you? What will you do now?"

I let out a heavy breath. "I'm not sure." I shake my head. "I never thought this would happen. They've been arrested. I feel I can relax, sort of."

Truthfully, I'm exhausted. I've been running around, thinking non-stop about what happened to my brother and who did it. Now that the men responsible are arrested, I can breathe.

I think of Mickey and can feel a tear welling from deep inside me. "I want to thank you as well, Detective," I say to him. "I know I'm not easy to deal with, but I feel you were listening to me. I wonder if others in your role would have as much patience."

He stands from his desk and comes around, shaking my hand. "I don't usually encourage people to do their own investigations, but if it wasn't for you, we may not be here. I'm curious, though, what do you think you'll do after university? You mentioned you're in your last year of criminology. Is law enforcement in your future?"

I smile. "Maybe I will become a lawyer someday. I'm not sure."

He nods. "Something tells me you'll excel at whatever you end up doing. You've got some perseverance to you, Ms. Roland. I wish you the best with your studies."

"I wish you the best with catching more bad guys." He smiles and opens his office door.

Before I leave, I turn to him. "Oh, one last thing."

"What's that?" he asks.

"My car's been totaled."

CHAPTER 41

Sister

It's over. My brother's killers have been arrested. Jenn came through, tying them to Mickey's death.

Despite everything working out so well, I still feel uneasy. A sick feeling in the pit of my stomach that I can't explain. I've felt this way ever since Drew dropped me off at the motel.

He offered to stay with me, but I declined.

As much as I want to spend time with him, I'm figuring out what I want to do now. I feel like I've been on a crusade the past few days to find my brother's killer and now that it's over, I don't like what's left.

Sadness.

The reality that my brother was killed. The reality that I'm truly alone now. My mother is dead. Brother killed. A biological father who's useless.

I feel like I'm on the verge of tears, and I hate myself for it. I don't want to feel this way. I hoped finding Mickey's killers would stop these feelings from coming, but now it's worse.

The dull pain of knowing you're all by yourself in life.

I have no family left. All I have is me.

I think of John's family and Melanie. They've been great to me. And even Drew is back in my life.

Despite that, being here in this motel makes me sick. Being in this town makes me ill. I can't stay here any longer. Being here reminds me how alone I am in this world.

At least in Toronto I have my studies. I have friends. I have a life.

All that's here is death and reminders of people I loved.

I manage a thin smile. Even my boyfriend is a mortician. I can't escape death.

Did I really think of Drew as my boyfriend just now?

I've looked for flights. I can catch the red eye tonight. While leaving town is all I want to do at this moment, I can't shake the sick feeling I have in the pit of my stomach.

Drew offered to drive me to the airport. I told him I wanted to handle the car rental first. I feel a last visit to the cemetery feels right as well.

Then there's John and his family. When I think of how I left his house, the sick feeling in my stomach gets worse.

It's ironic. Just how it was when I was younger, I can't wait to leave this town, but it feels like something is holding me back, only this time it's not Drew.

We talked about continuing to speak to each other after I go back, and I meant it. I know he does too.

So, on that front, I'm ready to leave, but something still doesn't feel right. I feel like I'm missing something.

As I finish packing up my belongings, my phone buzzes. When I answer it, the detective greets me.

"Any new updates?" I ask him. He said finding the

murder weapon would be the cherry on top for the case. I've been waiting patiently for his call the last few hours.

"Some good news," he admits. "We couldn't find the lamp or a key. Neither of them owns a shovel. But I spoke with the crown attorney about the case. He agrees we have a solid case. He's confident about going to trial with what we have."

"Well, that's good," I say.

"There's more," he continues. "They admitted to destroying your rental, and the windows at John's house and Ms. Harring's house."

"Even better," I say. That will certainly make the conversation with the car rental agency easier. I've been putting that talk off as long as I can.

"They're scared. They know it doesn't look good for them. They're trying their best to get us to believe them by telling us some truths but faking others. They still claim they didn't have anything to do with your brother's murder," he says. "Like I said, that won't matter. If that blood on the package we found at Jake's house belongs to your brother, we got them. Nothing they say will matter."

The uneasiness in my stomach gets worse as he says the words. "I'm worried. What if..."

"What?"

"What if they're telling the truth? Jenn says she never saw them at the crime scene until she called them."

The detective clears his throat. "The theory we have is that after they committed the murder, they were focused on... well, there's no nice way to put this. They were focused on cleaning up what they did. Disposing of your brother in the woods."

"What about their alibi?" I ask. "You told me the bartender at Woods Bar and Grill said Lenny and Jake were drinking there all night."

"That's what he said, sure. But we know these two aren't afraid to scare people to get them to do what they want."

I take a deep breath. "Okay."

"I don't want you to worry anymore, Sarah," he says, trying his best to comfort me with his confident tone. "This case is tight against both of them. Coupled with the drugs in their house, they won't have freedom again for a very long time. Both you and Jenn won't have to worry."

CHAPTER 42

Sister

When I open the rental driver's side door, I'm happy that I'm able to operate it without sitting on any glass. The entire back seat may be a huge mess, but the driver's side is fine after a little clean-up.

It may not look pretty rolling down, but the car is driveable. It took me a few YouTube videos to figure out how to put on a spare tire, but I was surprised how easy it was. Part of me wanted to call the agency to see if they could just tow it away.

I'm not sure if it's my stubbornness or embarrassment, but I struggle with calling them. I'm struggling with the idea of bringing it back to them in this condition.

Somehow, I know that despite having Lenny and Jake fess up to damaging the car, I'll get stuck with some kind of bill. The innocent victim charge.

If I was to call and ask for a tow, I'm sure there would be a fee for that as well. So I'll bring it by myself.

I've booked the red eye flight tonight from Calgary. Drew's going to drive me to the airport. We talked about having one last dinner together before I leave.

This won't be like last time. I won't accept him trying

to end things because of his fears of long-distance dating, so that I can move on, guilt-free.

Since coming back to Pinewood Springs, I've realized how important he is to me. He was the one I trusted to pick me up this morning when the car was damaged. He was the one I turned to when I needed help.

I'm not going to rush into anything with him. We'll take things slow. I do hope they go somewhere, though. Now that he's back in my life, I don't want to see him leave quickly.

I talk about this like I have it all sorted out. I don't even know how Drew really feels. Maybe he doesn't want to talk to me anymore. I dragged him through a murder investigation, after all.

This is not exactly the way one should rekindle an old relationship. After he left me at the motel, though, there was this awkward moment between us. I could tell from the look on his face that he wanted to kiss me again. It wasn't exactly the best time for it.

I'm looking forward to dinner tonight, though. I'm also looking forward to leaving this town behind me.

I turn on the ignition, but before I leave, I notice a crumpled picture that Melanie drew for me on the floor. I'm careful as I pick it up and smile, looking at the stick figures in the car. My grin grows wider when I see her stick figure penguin.

I'm seriously going to leave without saying goodbye to her? Without saying bye to John or Alice?

They opened their house to me, and what did I give back? A few rocks thrown through their windows. The way I left their home last night also bothers me. I don't want to leave things that way with Alice or John.

I need to see Melanie again.

I intend to pay John whatever it costs to reimburse him for his windows. I'm not sure why I'm being so avoidant of him and his family. It's almost like I feel guilty.

Guilty for the thoughts I had running in my mind the past few days. After I spotted John speaking to Jake and Lenny, my imagination ran wild with ideas that made no sense.

After seeing for myself how terrible my real father was, was I going to leave town without saying bye to the actual father who raised me?

"The key," I say out loud.

I open my purse and take out the key to John's house that he gave me. It's almost as if fate is telling me not to leave.

I have to say bye to him now. Melanie may not be my actual sister, but I really do love her. I love her enthusiasm. I love how much she loves life.

While I want to leave Pinewood Springs again, I don't want to forget about the people here. Drew, John. Alice and Melanie. These people matter to me.

I smile as I put John's housekey back into my purse. One more visit before leaving can't hurt. Maybe I'll be lucky and Alice will be cooking up something delicious and have enough for me to join them. The dinner with Drew will be much later tonight anyway. It will cut into our date time, but John and his family are important to me too.

Jake and Lenny were trying so hard to scare me out of town, but then no one could drag me out of here. Now I can't wait to leave. But before I do, I need to say goodbye to the people I care about.

The other benefit is I get to put off having a terrible

conversation with the rental car company for a little while longer.

CHAPTER 43

Sister

John's house is close to the motel, but the entire time, I'm worried a police officer will catch me riding in this vandalized car and I'll get a ticket.

Thankfully, I make it in one piece.

I wonder how many pages of Melanie's artwork I'll be able to take back to Toronto with me today. Hopefully a few more. John had joked that I'd have to buy another travel bag to bring all my gifts from her back to the city, but I managed to stuff them all into one suitcase.

I walk up the steps to their house and ring the doorbell. When I don't hear anyone inside, I knock on the door and it slightly opens.

How unlike John to not lock up his house properly, I think. I open it wider and call out for John and Alice, but nobody responds. I look at my cell for the time. It's eight at night.

Perhaps Alice took out Melanie for another of the nightly events she seems to have. Wasn't today her swimming day? I can't keep up with what she and Alice are up to.

John is likely at his store, plugging away at work as usual.

I should have called him before just popping by like this. If I want to make it on time for my late dinner with Drew and then my flight, I'll need to leave soon. I'm not even sure how long it will take with the rental car company. I imagine there'll be paperwork to fill.

"Hello?" I call into the empty house.

I take out my cell and dial John's number. It goes straight to voicemail. "Hey, John, it's Sarah. I'm really sorry about this. I was hoping to see you guys, but I have my flight tonight. I know it will likely be too late by the time you get this but if you want, you can meet up with Drew and me for dinner... Also, I have your housekey and I'll leave it in your kitchen before I leave. Your front door was unlocked when I got here, by the way."

I end the call and step into his house, closing the door behind me. As I head toward the kitchen, I can't help but stop and look into Melanie's craft area. I see a new picture she was working on. In this picture are two curly-haired stick figures holding hands. Above the shorter one she wrote "me" and on the other side "sister."

I smile. I'm very tempted to take the picture home with me but I can imagine how upset Melanie may be if her artwork is suddenly missing when she gets home. She may think John threw another one away.

I'm starting to feel vile for leaving before having a proper goodbye with her. I let my emotions from the week play out and I'm ready to leave because I'm so drained. All I want is to go back to Toronto, and surprisingly, back to school.

I'm actually looking forward to it.

I haven't been away too long. I'll be able to make up the time without having to take a semester off.

I walk into the kitchen. I've seen Alice and John toss

their keys in one of the drawers before. I open the first one but it's full of random items. When I open the drawer beside it, I spot several keys. Before I place the one in my hand to join the rest, I see it.

The key I've been looking for. The key that was supposed to be in the fake rock. I pick up the key with the Calgary Flames emblem on it in amazement, examining it as if it's not real. My mouth drops open as I start to make the connections.

Suddenly, the back door opens and Alice comes inside with headphones on. She's wearing stained white gloves and has a garden shovel in her hand.

Her face drops when she sees me, and she covers her chest. "Sarah! You scared me." She laughs. "What are you doing?" I hold the key as if it's a grenade. When I turn to her with it in my hand she looks at me, confused. "What are you doing?" she asks again.

"Did you use this?" I ask, dumbfounded by what I have I found in their drawer and the implications that come with it.

Alice raises an eyebrow. "No, what's the key for?"

"Was John using it?"

She looks even more puzzled. "I don't understand."

I try to calm my breathing, but my heart is about to burst out of my chest. "Where's John?"

"Out with Melanie," she says. "He wanted to take her swimming tonight. It gave me some time to garden."

I take another deep breath. "I need to call the police."

"Over a key?" Alice says, confused. "What's wrong, Sarah?" Her phone buzzes in her pocket. She takes it out and looks. "It's John."

"Don't tell him I'm here," I plead. "Don't pick up."

She laughs. "What's come over you? Let's just talk

whatever this is out, okay? You're kind of scaring me."

I'm sure the shock on my face is apparent, but Alice has no clue why the key in my hands holds so much relevance. It's the key to Mickey's back door. It was the key used to get inside my brother's house. It's how his killer murdered him without breaking in.

Lenny and Jake were telling the truth. It was John.

John killed Mickey.

I turn to the side window looking at the driveway. "What time is John coming back?" I ask. Alice doesn't answer me.

When I turn to her, the garden shovel is above her head, her face full of rage. I'm paralyzed with fear as she swings it down onto me.

CHAPTER 44

Sister

With my eyes rolling and my head pounding, I call out again for help. I've woken up in a dark, confined area. After some time, I realize I'm in the trunk of a car.

I can hear the driver listening to music. I've called out for help, but the driver doesn't reply. Instead, I hear what sounds like a voice coming from inside the dark trunk.

"Who's there?" I call out.

"Sarah," a whispered voice says. "Sarah, stay awake."

My eyes roll back in my head, and I feel so sleepy. I reach out towards the voice but no one's there. "Help me," I say. "Help me!" I yell.

"Be quiet back there!" the driver shouts.

As my eyes close, a voice in the trunk speaks to me. It's barely audible, but someone else is here with me. "Alice," the voice says.

"Alice!" I shout.

"Shut up!" the driver screams. "Shut up! Shut up!"

Although my memory is foggy, her voice registers with me.

"Alice!" I call out to her. "Please, help me!"

"Shut up!" she replies. "This is not my fault! This is

all your brother's doing! He had to take and take and take from John and me. I need you to know, I didn't want to kill him. I just wanted to hurt him. All the time he called and asked for money, and my dumb husband did as he asked. Why? I blame your mother too! He still loves her. She's been dead and buried for years and he still loves her. He still loves her children! What about me? What about our marriage? Mickey was never going to pay us back! He was going to keep taking!"

I try my best to focus on her words, but it's difficult. All I want to do is close my eyes.

"Stay awake!" a clear voice from the trunk calls out to me in the dark. "Pull the cord," it whispers.

"Cord?" I say confused. "What? Who's there?"

"Cord!" the voice yells.

My eyes shut for a moment, until the car rolls over a speed bump, waking me. "Alice!" I shout to my captor. "Please, don't hurt me."

"I told you to shut up!" Alice shrieks. "I didn't want to kill you! I didn't want to. You had to keep nosing around town. You had to keep playing detective. You are too stubborn for your own good, Sarah! Your brother died because he was a no-good junkie. You're going to die because you were too stupid to quit searching for answers! None of this is my fault!"

In the darkness of the trunk, I move my hand around, trying to find a way to escape.

"Cord!" the voice says again.

I blink several times and see a neon cord hanging near my feet. My eyes fix on it, and I try to reach out, but I can't touch it. I curl my body in, trying to shuffle around to grab at it. My hand nearly touches it for a moment. The neon cord swings in the darkness as my eyes continue to roll to the back of my head. I put a hand to my forehead, trying my best to focus.

"I'm not a bad person!" Alice shouts from the driver's seat. "This is *your* fault!"

I reach out again for the cord as the voice calls out for me to keep trying. "I am trying," I say. My mouth gapes open, and drool falls onto my forearm. I wipe it away. That's when I realize my fingers are sticky.

Am I sweating? The substance on my hands is much too sticky for it to be sweat. It hits me that it's my own blood. I feel a stinging sensation in my skull as I realize how hurt I am.

I look at the neon cord again as my eyes begin to shut.

"Stay awake!" the voice demands. "Stay awake! Sarah!"

Alice starts to yell something at me, but now the words are unrecognizable. Everything sounds muffled, except the voice that yells at me to stay awake and keep trying to reach the cord.

"Sarah! Don't sleep!"

CHAPTER 45

Brother

"Wake up, Sarah!" I shout to my sister as her eyes shut and do not open. "Wake up!"

It's useless, though. Her body stops fighting and completely shuts down. I go up to her, barely able to see her in the dark. I put my head near her lips, hoping to see her nostrils flare, or her chest inhale. I need to see some sign that she's still alive.

As I continue to search for one, my eyes grow wide, listening to Alice from the driver's chair. "I'm not a bad person! This is your fault. It's Mickey's fault. It's John's fault!"

John's fault?

The woman has completely lost it. How can she blame others for what she's about to do? What she has already done.

With the dim light of the neon cord illuminating my sister's body, I continue to hope, pray, that she's okay. Alice stops the vehicle suddenly. I'm scared that she'll turn off the car and open the trunk. If she does, I won't be able to protect Sarah. I won't be able to do anything but watch as Alice kills my sister.

"I hate you!" I shout at her, but she doesn't respond.

Instead, the car starts to drive again. I realize that she must have been at a red light.

I look down at my sister and in the darkness see her throat pulse. I let out a laugh. She's alive... for now.

"We need to escape," I tell her. "Wake up, sis." I try to shake her, but my hands go through her body. She moves for a moment as I do. "You heard me before. You must sense me. Now, get up!" I try to move her body with my hands, but they continue to pass through her.

Her breathing gets heavier, and I realize she's completely out of it.

"You're so close, Sarah. Just wake up and reach for the cord."

I look at the neon cord that glows in the dark. On it is an image of a stick figure man getting out of a trunk. It was almost comical when I saw the cord in the dark. The image represented everything I wanted to happen. Sarah needed to pull the cord for the trunk to release so she could escape.

I look down at my sister who's still knocked out. She'll live through the car ride, but Alice won't stop there.

She won't let Sarah live after seeing what she saw.

I wonder what I looked like when Alice was disposing of my body.

It hits me suddenly. I'm still present, even though Sarah's not conscious. How is that possible?

Since I've returned, I've been connected to my sister. If Drew's story about his grandmother was to be taken literally, Sarah's love for me brought me back. She needed me by her side. She needed my support to find out the truth.

Wherever Sarah went, I physically had to follow. Whenever she sleeps, I rest, until she wakes. Not now, though. She's unable to help herself, and yet I'm still here.

"This is not my fault!" Alice shouts in the front seat, enraging me further.

Then it hits me.

I realize why I'm still here now. I'm no longer connected to Sarah. No. Now I'm tied to the one who killed me.

I close my eyes and when I open them, I'm in the backseat of Alice's car. She shakes her head as she drives down the highway. The trees on either side of the road make the route more narrow.

"The stupid key!" Alice says with gritted teeth. "Stupid key!" She bangs on the steering wheel again. "I forgot it was there. I was so scared after..." She turns her head and looks past me, toward the trunk. "Blame your brother for this! If he wasn't such a junkie, mooching off everyone else, destroying other lives, not just his own, you wouldn't be in there!"

Alice takes a deep breath. "I got rid of his body. I got rid of the damn lamp. How? How could I forget about the key! I put it in the drawer with the rest of the keys like a moron! I just wanted to be happy with Melanie and John, and he ruined everything for us!"

Her words hit me. Suddenly, my anger softens as she reminds me about who I was when I was alive.

I lean over the back of her chair and place my lips near her ear. "I'm sorry, Alice. I wish I wasn't such a screw-up. Now that I see things so clearly, I know I messed up. I know I impacted your family. I impacted you. I took money from you. I didn't spend it on drugs, though. I actually tried to get help. I did. I just failed... I'm a screw-up. I know. I didn't want to be. I just was. I wish I could have done better. I do. I loved Melanie, though. I loved our talks together. I loved feeling like I had a family with you, her and John." I lower my head and try my best to reason with her. "Don't do this. Please. Turn the car around. Drive my sister to the hospital. She needs help, immediately. There's still time. Please."

Alice ignores me but suddenly starts to drive faster down the highway.

"Please, Alice. Don't do something you'll regret. Don't be a screw-up like me. Think of Melanie."

Alice crosses the yellow line to the other lane to pass a slower vehicle.

"Alice! Go back! Now!" I demand.

She waves her hand beside her ear as if I'm a fly buzzing near her. She doesn't hear me, but I can tell she senses me.

"I'm a good person," she whispers.

I nod. "You can still be a good person, Alice. The hospital isn't far from here. We can make it on time to save Sarah. Don't mess up in life like me." I lower my head and take a moment, trying to find the words. I look at Alice through the rearview mirror. Her eyes are wet as she continues to speed down the highway. "I can forgive you for what you did to me, Alice. Just don't hurt my sister."

She continues to ignore me, but for a moment, she looks in my direction in the mirror.

"I hate you!" I shout in her ear as loud as I can. Again, Alice acts like I'm some sort of bug near her ear and tries to wave me away.

As she drives, I see a sign for Pinewood Springs National Park.

"So that's where you're taking her," I say. "The same place you took me."

She's going to drag her body through the woods like

she did with mine. She'll take Sarah off-trail somewhere and leave her. I'm sure this time she won't go so close to the river where some old hiker and his dog will find her body.

My eyes widen as I make another connection. I shake my head in disbelief as I look behind me. The answer as to who killed me was there the whole time. From the first day I came back, had I paid attention, I would have known who killed me.

Melanie was telling us the whole time.

"Mickey. Back. Sleeping."

Those were the words she said over and over. She even drew pictures. She drew many, many pictures. All of them had her and her mother, both with sad faces. I was the stick figure in the back, behind Melanie. The stupid penguins threw me off, but Melanie was trying to tell us.

Mickey was in the back. Mickey was in the trunk.

Mickey was sleeping?

I look at Alice, my mouth gaping open. "Melanie saw me the day you killed me, didn't she?" She continues to drive down the narrow road.

I shake my head in disbelief. "Melanie wasn't with you when you snuck up behind me and killed me, was she?" I ask. "No, you wouldn't have done that... I hope. She must have seen you put me in the trunk, though... You told her I was *sleeping?*"

I can feel my rage building inside me as I think of Melanie unknowingly seeing my dead body.

"How could you do that?" I say. "How could you do this to me?" I look at my hands. As I get more enraged, my skin starts to turn grey. Open sores start appearing along my arms. My clothes start to rip.

"You did this to me," I say to her. "*You* did this!" I

shout at the top of my lungs.

Alice turns her head as I shout, looking in the backseat.

"You can hear me," I say. "You know I'm here."

Alice quickly looks back at the road, weaving into the other lane momentarily.

I laugh. "You killed me, Alice! You did this to me. You. You're the one who needs to take responsibility for their actions!"

A piece of flesh from my face falls from my cheek. I can see the flap of my skin from the corner of my eye.

I'm turning into what I looked like after I was killed. After Alice murdered me.

"Look at what you did, Alice!" I shout, attempting to put my arms on her shoulder. "Look at me!"

Alice looks at the rearview mirror, and for a moment, our eyes meet. I can see the fear in her eyes. I smile as she becomes more terrified. Alice shrieks and the car weaves.

"You did this!" I shout. "You!"

Alice stares at me wide eyed through the rearview mirror, a hand over her chest as she screams in terror. She's completely lost control of the vehicle, letting go of the wheel. The car veers sharply to the side of the road, smashing into a tree.

Alice lets out a gush of breath as a large branch breaks through the windshield and impales her through the chest.

"You did this," I say, as I watch her take her last breaths and the life goes out of her eyes. I can see my terrifying reflection in them as she passes.

I know when she's completely dead, I'll no longer be here. I won't exist any longer.

I look behind me, knowing Sarah is still in the trunk,

trapped and unconscious.

"I'm sorry," I whisper. When I close my eyes, all I see is black.

CHAPTER 46

Brother

Life is funny.

I can't help but think of this phrase as I watch over my sister as the beeps of the machine connected to her remind me she's still alive.

She's doing much better now. At first, hospital staff were worried about the extent of her traumatic brain injury, but she's been recovering nicely.

I stand beside her bed in the dark room. Any light still bothers her quite a bit. The doctors have told her that this will pass though.

None of that is funny, of course. What I find humorous, however, is how my sister was discovered in the trunk.

An old man and his dog named Peaches were driving along the highway when they found Alice's car smashed into the tree at the side of the road.

If the old hiker didn't stop to check, I'm certain my sister would have joined me days ago.

Thankfully, that wasn't the case.

Besides the concussion, Sarah's injuries were minor, especially when compared to Alice' fatal ones. Sarah had a few broken ribs and a scratched-up leg but was otherwise fine. Alice, and the front of the car, took the most damage. Oddly enough, being in a confined area in the trunk helped Sarah avoid the worst.

I look much better myself. My skin is of a normal color. No more bruises or open sores. My face appears intact again. Whatever gruesome sight I turned into in Alice's car is now gone.

Sarah turns a page in the book she's reading. It's about the only thing she can do that doesn't give her a headache. She tried watching television but immediately asked the nurse to turn it off since it was bothering her.

Being in a dark room, watching my sister read all day, has been the most boring days of my afterlife, but all I care about, of course, is that she's safe.

I've been left to my own thoughts. I can't get what happened in Alice's car out of my mind. I knew she was going to kill Sarah, but I also thought there was nothing I could do about it.

I was wrong.

I've had time to mull this over and think about why Sarah and Alice are the only two people who could sense my presence. One was the only person left in the world who truly loved me, and the other was my killer.

That can't be a coincidence.

A knock on the door causes Sarah to lower her book. When she sees who it is, she can't hide the grin on her face.

"Hey," Drew says, taking a step inside the room. He's got a large bunch of roses with a teddy bear in his hand.

"For me?" Sarah says with a funny tone.

Drew shakes his head. "Nope." He looks around the hospital room. "I must have mixed up my room numbers." He comes in and places the flowers and bear on a stand beside her bed, along with the other flowers.

The other bouquet was from John and Melanie. John dropped them off himself but didn't stay long to talk.

I don't blame him. I can only imagine what he's going through after finding out what Alice did.

Now he's a two-time widower.

I try not to think about what Alice's death will mean for Melanie. Knowing John, though, I think she'll be okay.

"How are you feeling today?" Drew asks my sister.

She nods. "Better. I think they're going to let me go soon."

"I can give you a ride when they discharge you," Drew says. "I can drop you off at your family home."

Sarah shakes her head. "I don't want to go back there. Would it be okay if I stayed at your place for a few days?"

Drew nods. "Of course."

I roll my eyes. "Here we go again." I'm okay with not being part of this blossoming love story.

I've been in this room with my sister since they brought her here and she was awake. Besides me, Drew's been here nearly just as much.

When I see them talk, I know how much love Sarah has for him. I can also feel the love from Drew as well.

I'm not sure if this will be a happily ever after for them, though. At some point, Sarah will go back to university. Drew will go back to the cemetery, spending his days with more people like me.

They will go back to how it was before Sarah came back to town.

Drew leans down and kisses her softly. "I'm just so happy you're doing better," he says. "I was so scared when I found out."

"Who told you about me being here?" Sarah asks.

"John called," Drew says. "He's been a wreck over everything but still called me. I'm glad he did." Drew grabs my sister's hand and holds it tightly in his.

As I watch them, I wonder if I'm wrong. Maybe they'll find a way to stay together this time.

I hope they do.

A nurse knocks on the door and walks into the room. "Just taking a look at your vitals again," she says looking over the machine and making notes on her pad. "I spoke with the doctor and he's thinking of maybe discharging you tonight or tomorrow morning. Would that be okay?"

Sarah smiles at Drew and answers the nurse. "That's great news."

I watch as the nurse leaves. When I turn back to my sister, Drew is playfully flirting with her and the two kiss again.

For a change, their embrace makes me smile. "Take care of her, Drew," I say. I walk up to the door, and this time, I'm able to step straight into the hallway. Not only that, but I can also move out of sight of my sister.

Whatever force was causing me to never leave her side appears to be gone now.

As I continue down the hall, I realize I'm free to leave. I go back to my sister's room to have one more look at her.

As I watch her and Drew talk to each other, I feel it's time for me to leave her side. "I love you, Sarah," I say. When I feel ready, I head down the hall towards an exit sign.

I'm not exactly sure what I'll do now. I feel my time here in Pinewood Springs is done. I'm ready to leave.

"Michael," a woman's voice calls out to me.

I'm about to correct her to say "Mickey" when I realize the woman is talking to me.

"Michael," the familiar voice says again. This time I hear her directly behind me.

When I look, the hallway is bright. It's as if the sun is shining through the dim halls of the hospital. In the brightest part of the light in front of me, I hear her voice again. "Michael, you can come with me now."

Suddenly the bright light takes the shape of a woman. No longer is she sick and skinny from the cancer that killed her. She's just as beautiful as ever.

She reaches out for me, and I grab her hand. Instead of going through her, though, I feel her warm, soft skin on mine.

I smile as I stare at her. "Mom."

CHAPTER 47

Sister

I walk down a path, hand in hand with Drew. He stops suddenly, and gives me a kiss, whispering how much he loves me. Even though I've been hearing him say it for some time, I still can't get enough of it.

When he said the words on the day he proposed to me, only a few months ago, my heart fluttered. Today, it still flutters.

After I was discharged from the hospital, I spent a few more days in town, mostly with Drew. He said he wanted to keep in touch after I left. I jokingly asked him if he was going to leave me again when I went back to Toronto.

He said it was a mistake when he first left me and would never do it again, given another chance.

I never thought that chance would happen so quickly. As I finished my senior year at university, he made plans to leave Pinewood Springs to join me in Toronto.

He was right when he said he could find work as a mortician easily. He found a new job within a few weeks of moving.

Things felt almost how they were when we dated

years ago. I was just as infatuated with him as I was when I was younger.

I followed up with Detective Drayson a while ago. From what I understand, Jenn Harring's life is also on a much better path. She's been clean and sober for nearly a year. I couldn't help myself and one day looked her up on her social media. I saw her arm wrapped around a handsome man in one of her recent profile pictures. She seems to have found happiness as well.

Life is certainly not perfect for Jake Matthews and Lenny Mercer, though. While they were not my brother's murderers, they still committed many crimes on the day of his death, along with the drugs found on their properties. They're facing some serious jail time.

I always felt Jake was the smarter one of the duo. Lenny took a plea deal for his charges and will be out of jail within eight years. Jake, though, tried to talk his way out of prison and had the audacity to be his own attorney. He's looking at fifteen years now.

After I recovered from my concussion and was out of the hospital, John was nervous about seeing me. He felt terrible after what happened. His wife murdered my brother. She was going to kill me next. John had no idea what Alice was truly capable of.

I'm convinced that Alice wasn't aware either. Somehow, I know that her murdering Mickey was not planned. In my heart, I believe she did it out of impulse. In the heat of the moment, her rage got the best of her. Mickey had become a burden to her because of John. John wasn't going to give up on Mickey. He would have continued to help him. Alice had had enough.

It took some time before John and I were able to talk to each other again. One day, he randomly texted me to ask if it would be okay for him to call, and I agreed. I wanted to speak to him. I wanted to talk to Melanie as well.

I watch as John and Melanie hold hands, walking ahead of us down the path. Melanie was ecstatic when she found out Drew and I were coming back to Pinewood Springs for a visit. She literally jumped up and down with joy when we went to John's house and asked Melanie if she wanted to go on a day trip to the zoo.

We spent an exorbitant amount of time with the penguins.

Thankfully, Melanie allowed us to view other animals today. She seemed to enjoy the hippopotamus and the monkeys. I wonder if in a few days she'll start drawing stick figure hippos beside her penguins.

As we walked around the large zoo and the sun was beginning to set, Melanie insisted we go back to see the penguins again before leaving. Since their enclosure is by the exit, John said it was okay but reminded her that the zoo would be closing soon. John made Melanie promise not to be upset when it was time to go.

As John and Melanie stand beside the clear wall that looks into the penguin exhibit, Drew grabs my hands and leans into me. "Are you going to ask?"

I take a deep breath. "I know. I should have done it at the beginning of the day."

"You still want to ask him, right?"

I nod. "I do. I guess... I'm nervous."

Drew laughs. "I think you're the most courageous person I know. Just do it. Like a band-aid. Quick."

I laugh. "Okay."

"I'll distract Melanie," Drew says with a wink. He saunters up beside Melanie and points at one of animals.

"Melanie, do you know what kind of penguin that one is called?"

She smiles at him and nods. "Yes! Emperor penguin."

Drew's face lights up. "That's correct! Before we came here, I learned a few facts about that type of penguin. Did you know that the emperor penguin is the tallest of all the penguins in the whole wide world?"

Melanie's face drops. "No. I didn't," she says with a serious tone.

Drew smiles. "That's right. I learned more facts. Can I tell you about them?" Melanie nods vigorously. Drew laughs and turns his head, winking at me.

John laughs as well. "Drew, this is all she will want to talk about with you now."

Drew nods. "I'm prepared."

"Tell me more!" Melanie shouts.

I take a deep breath to try and collect myself, before walking up to the other side of John. "Hey, can we talk for a moment?"

John's smile quickly vanishes. "Yeah, sure." He takes a few steps away from Melanie and Drew as they continue their conversation. "Is everything okay?" he asks, concerned.

"It is," I say, hopefully comforting his worries. "I had a question for you." He waits patiently for me to ask. "So, Drew and I, our marriage will be in Toronto, but I'm hoping you and Melanie will be there."

John smiles. "Of course. We wouldn't miss it for anything. Melanie has been telling people at school how her sister is getting married soon."

I feel a tear well up and do my best to stay composed. "That's so nice to hear," I say. "Well, that wasn't exactly my question, though." I lower my head. "I don't know why this is so hard for me to ask. You and Melanie… you guys are the only family I have left now. I was hoping… would you be willing to walk me down the aisle?"

When I look back at John, he has tears of his own now. He grins and nods. "Of course. I'd love to."

I smile. "That's not all." I catch a tear in my eye and quickly wipe it, although I'm sure John noticed. "I know I'm in my twenties now, but… well, I already call Melanie my sister. Would it be okay if I started calling you Dad?"

John tries his best to conceal his tears but is failing miserably as well. "I'd love that, Sarah." He puts out his hands, and he hugs me tightly. "Your mom would be happy to see us now. Mickey too."

I smile. "They would be."

A loud voice comes over the speaker in the penguin exhibit. "Thank you for visiting the Calgary Zoo. We hope you enjoyed your day. This is a reminder that we will be closing in fifteen minutes. Please start heading towards the exit, and we hope to see you again."

Melanie looks around, confused, and stomps her feet. "No!"

EPILOGUE

Sister

After we spend the day with Melanie and John, we visit the rest of my family.

We took our time at my mother's grave. I've brought flowers for her and place them below her stone. I kiss my hand and place it on the cold rock.

Next, we visit Mickey's grave. Mickey was never a flower kind of guy, so instead Drew and I stand in silence in front of his resting place.

After a while, I look at Drew. "Is it okay if I have a little time alone?"

Drew nods. "Of course." He points towards the nearby building. "I saw an old coworker's car in the lot when we came in."

I laugh. "I will never get over how many friends you've made at a cemetery."

I wait for him to leave before I speak to my brother. I lower my head, trying to find the words. I thought about what I would say to him all day when I visited his grave, but now that I'm here, nothing is coming out.

"I hope you're with Mom now," I tell Mickey. "I hope the two of you are together." I look up at the sunny sky and smile. "I hope, some day, I'll see you both again."

I think of the last time I was in Pinewood Springs. I think about the strong feelings I had when I tried to solve what happened to my brother for myself. I also think of my fiancé's story he shared about his grandmother and how he felt her presence after she passed.

"You were with me the whole time, weren't you?" I say to his tombstone. I shake my head in disbelief at what I'm saying. "You were with me when Alice had me in the trunk... I had a nasty concussion, but I heard you. I heard your voice, didn't I? You were watching out for me." I lower my head. "Were you the reason Alice crashed?"

I look around the cemetery, thinking that if anyone heard me right now they'd think I'm completely insane. Maybe I am. I think about what happened with Alice often. I think about waking up in her trunk, completely out of it. I think about the voice I heard in the darkness. The voice that tried to keep me alive.

Mickey was with me. Just as Drew felt his grandmother, Mickey was with me in that trunk. The police, Drew, everyone feels I was just lucky to have survived what happened. They assume that in her moment of madness, Alice flew off the highway on purpose.

It wasn't luck or her mental health though.

Someone was watching out for me. Some people call them guardian angels. It's weird to think Mickey could have such a role.

I scoff at my own thoughts. "I'm so stupid sometimes." I laugh.

There were times I felt so strongly that Micky was with me after he passed. Just like Drew's story, though, those feelings left me. No longer did I sense his presence.

I take a deep breath, staring at his tombstone.

Suddenly it hits me that my family are all dead.

"Now I'm truly alone," I say to myself. Tears begin to well up from deep inside me.

I may have Drew in my life. And Melanie and John too. But my mother and brother are no longer with me.

"It's not fair," I whisper, as I stare at his tombstone. "It's just not fair."

My brother won't be able to attend my wedding. He would have no doubt been a complete goofball the entire time and likely driving me crazy, but I wish he could have. Mom won't be able to come and see me say "I do" to the love of my life.

It's not fair.

As my tears fall freely, a weird sensation comes over me. Gusts of wind blow my hair. A warm feeling starts in my heart and covers my entire body like a cozy blanket. For a moment, I feel a presence. Actually, more than one this time.

I know it's not real. My mind plays tricks on me to comfort me when I'm sad, but I imagine Mickey and my mother's arms around me, telling me everything will be okay.

I manage to smile and wipe away my tears.

"I love you, Mom. I love you, Mickey."

* * *

Note from the author:

I truly hope you enjoyed reading my story as much as I did creating it. As an indie author, what you think of my book is all I care about.

If you enjoyed my story, please take a moment to leave your review on Amazon. It would mean the world to me.

Thank you for reading, and I hope you join me next time.

Sincerely,
James

Download My Free Book

If you would like to receive a FREE copy of my psychological thriller, The Affair, email me at jamescaineauthor@gmail.com.

I'm always happy to hear from readers.

Thanks again,
James

Now, please enjoy a sample of my book, The Couple at the Lake House.

THE COUPLE AT THE LAKE HOUSE

You're invited to the lake house.

When newly engaged Sidney is out on a date with her fiancé, she runs into an old flame, Cole, and his girlfriend. Initially, Sidney resists when Cole invites them to join his table but when the couples hit it off, she sets aside her reservations.

Soon after, Cole's invitation extends to a stay at their remote lake house.

What starts as a picturesque weekend unravels into a chilling nightmare when misunderstandings turn to paranoia and tensions reach a boiling point.

Sidney tries to escape when she realizes the truth.
Leaving was never an option.

PROLOGUE

After speaking to the 911 operator, I hang up. I pace the kitchen back and forth, the weight of the call heavy on my mind. Adrenaline is rampaging through my body. I just want to run away from here. What if I'm not here when the authorities arrive?

In my daze, I realize the gun is still gripped tightly in my hand. I place it on the kitchen counter, and stare at it.

What have I done?

I take a deep breath and try to calm my thoughts. It's impossible given what happened.

I look around the beautifully decorated house and the scenic views of the lake from the large windows. Its beauty would touch anyone. I will be happy to never see such a view ever again.

I can't leave, though. That will only make things much worse. I must wait for the authorities to come. I feel stuck.

I told the emergency dispatcher everything. Well, most of it.

I wonder how the police will react when they arrive and discover what's happened. Will I feel the cold steel of their cuffs on my hands when they do?

I lower my head and try to calm myself. It doesn't work. My eyes widen and my face tightens as I see the bloodstains on my shirt.

"Sidney," a faint voice calls out to me. I raise my head, hoping I'm hearing things.

Please let me be delusional. Please let me be crazy. This can't be happening.

It was supposed to be a fun weekend. How could it ever have turned into this?

"Sidney," the voice says again. "Help me." Walking to the stairs, I look up and see the source of what's haunting me. "Please, Sidney."

CHAPTER 1

"We want to thank Sidney Meyers for her presentation today!" Vanessa Fleming yells to the crowd. The people watching me stand up from their chairs and clap. I'm bad at guessing, but I'd say there's nearly two hundred people in the room.

"Thanks," I say to Vanessa. She smiles at me. Vanessa knows it went well. We were both worried when I stood on stage that it would be a disaster. My behaviour over the past year would have made anyone worried. Vanessa is one of the main editors for my publisher, Twisted Thriller Books. She's also my main contact with my publisher. I never wanted to come to this event. I threatened not to, but my publisher then threatened to stop sending me my royalties.

I look back at the crowd who continue to clap. "Thank you all for coming today," I say.

On the large screen behind me is an image of my bestseller, *My Life as a Killer*. When I wrote it, it was more for fun. I never thought a publisher would pick it up. I was willing to self-publish it but was amazed when Twisted Thriller Books accepted my submission. A book where the main character is a serial killer, living in a regular neighborhood, amongst normal people, would not typically be a huge seller. People loved my idea of a psychologist who's an actual psychopath who murders and lies her way through everyday life.

Most authors will tell you that your main character needs to be likeable or relatable. Well, my book blows conventional wisdom out of the water.

My main character, Tracy Macher, is a killer. She's a terrible person who does terrible things. Yet readers loved to read about her. They were fascinated with her, wondered why she did the things she did. I think what many people wanted to read, though, was her eventual downfall. How would Tracy get caught?

In my story, she didn't.

My publisher tried to talk me out of the ending I wrote. They wanted Tracy to be discovered. For justice to prevail. I somehow won the argument, fully expecting the criticisms readers would have. But they loved it. I was surprised myself. I never expected it would bring me to where I am now, in front of a large group of fans at a huge writing convention in Toronto, Canada.

I never thought that anything I did in my life would lead to a room full of people clapping because of something I did. I smile and try my best to take in the moment.

When I agreed to be the keynote speaker at Readers Unite, I knew I'd struggle. My publisher reminded me of the obligations I had when I signed with them. When I showed resistance to holding up my end of the bargain, I received a letter from my publisher. The letter was full of fluffy legal terms but what they wanted was clear. Promote the book we published, or else.

My entire life changed when Twisted Thriller Books agreed to publish my book. I had written a few stories in the past, but none of them came even close to the amount of attention *My Life as a Killer* received.

I'm not sure why it's become so popular. When I asked my editor, Vanessa, how this could have happened, she couldn't answer. She did tell me one thing, though: write another one.

Easier said than done.

"And now," Vanessa continues, "we have a few minutes for questions from the crowd."

I smile. Oh gee, my favorite part. In my head I worry that I'll completely freeze if someone asks me a question that I didn't see coming. Thankfully, they never seem to.

This crowd is the same. How did I come up with the idea for *My Life as a Killer*? Which authors influenced my work? How did I start writing? They're all the same questions and I tend to give the same answers.

A man wearing a Hawaiian shirt stands up to the microphone the crew set up in the aisle. "Hey, Sidney, I'm such a fan," he says, his voice a little shaky. He's obviously nervous. If only he knew how nervous I am being the one he's talking to as well.

"Thank you," I say with a warm smile.

"I'm your biggest fan," he continues. My face drops when he says the line. I try to hide my fear at how he said it. I'm not sure why it triggered me the way it did. I take a deep breath and recover the grin I had before. "I even have a few of your books autographed," he says, the shakiness in his voice leaving him now that he feels more confident. "My question for you, though, is, I need more of you." Some of the crowd laughs. "I do," the man says. "When is your next book coming out?"

I smile. This is another common question. I have an answer ready for it, but no matter how many times I'm asked, it always makes me feel like complete garbage. "I'm working closely with my editor and publisher," I say.

"There's no set timeframe right now, but I hope it's sooner rather than later. Thank you so much for reading my stories and I'm so happy that you and everyone in this room is enjoying them."

He smiles as I answer. "Any hint about what it's about?" he asks.

I pull a pretend zipper across my mouth. "My editor will kill me if I say." The crowd laughs at my terrible joke.

Vanessa stands beside me. "That's all the time we have, folks," she says. "Sidney will be staying for a short while if anyone wants autographs." The crowd cheers for me again as I thank them all for coming. I stare at the man in the crowd who asked the question and he's clapping the hardest of everyone.

None of the answer I gave the shirt guy was true. I haven't been working with my editor at all. She would love it if I was though. They would love a sequel to *My Life as a Killer*. I just can't though.

I have a general idea of what to write about, and because my publisher wants to keep me, they agreed to the idea. What they really want is to talk me into writing the sequel.

The truth is I haven't written anything of substance in over a year. I try to give myself grace. Not everyone would even want to continue writing after what happened to me. I take in the crowd's smiles, cheers and claps and remind myself that I deserve my success.

If only they knew what happened. If only they knew how I wish I was never at this convention. Would they still clap for me?

CHAPTER 2

After the event is over, Vanessa rushes me over to a smaller room, where a table with piles of my books is waiting for me. Behind the table is a large banner with an image of me smiling, holding a copy of *My Life as a Killer*.

I'm smiling confidently in the photo. I remember how happy I was when my publisher sent a photographer to my home to take it. My world was spinning. I thought I could conquer the world back then. My book was already a best-selling hit. Sales have only increased since.

I had written a few books before, but with my newest release, I had become an overnight success. I had done interviews, podcasts, and contributed to written articles about my book.

My life changed entirely. Who was it that said money doesn't solve anything? It most certainly did... at first.

I was able to buy a new car within a few months. An upgrade from my beat-up Volkswagen that was on its last legs. Next, I paid off my debt, which was substantial at the time. I was over thirty and I still had debt from university from my Bachelor of English program and other terrible expenditures I had in my twenties. After eight months, I'd saved up a substantial downpayment for a new home.

My fiancé, Matt, was ecstatic! We could live in a beautiful house right away after we married. The problem was, when could we marry? Matt had a large extended family. He was used to big weddings and parties. I never cared for them myself. I'd rather have a small intimate group of friends and family at ours, but Matt was different. It was stereotypes in reverse. He wanted his dream wedding, and he wouldn't settle for less for our big day.

Sometimes I think everything about our relationship was in reverse. Matt was more romantic than me. He actually enjoyed cheesy romance movies and would make suggestions on what we should watch together. The man was a clean freak. He would be the one giving me crap about not putting the dishes in the sink or for not folding the pile of laundry in the closet that belonged to me.

Even though he made decent money as an accountant, I was the breadwinner now with my newfound success. He was happy about that, but looking back, I should have known better. Matt was never the type to tell me what he was thinking or feeling. He kept it all inside until one night when he'd just freak out on me for an accumulation of things I had forgotten to do.

When the publishers asked me to do book tours for *My Life as a Killer*, they understood that I wanted to limit myself at first, because the wedding was planned around the same time. Matt was the one who encouraged me to do the tour, and we would push back our wedding date. I told him our marriage was more important, but he explained that this was a once in a lifetime opportunity. I needed to see this through. How many authors would kill to be in my position right now?

We pushed back our wedding date and now it was to be determined. We still haven't set a date. I tried to get him to change his mind about having a large wedding.

Large weddings took time, and with the popularity of my book and my publisher on my back to write another one quickly, I didn't have it.

Then, everything happened to me, and life has been a disaster ever since.

I sit at the table and take a deep breath. I turn my head and the taller printed version of myself is mocking me with her smile.

Isn't this what I wanted?

Vanessa comes up and offers me a bottle of water. I thank her profusely as I open it and take a sip. Some of it spills on my blouse and I quickly wipe it away. I shouldn't have worn this material. The water stain is larger after I tried to clean it.

Great. Just what I need. I'm already anxious enough. Now people will know I don't know how to drink properly.

Vanessa asks if I'm ready and I nod. "Yes, you can let people in."

She walks over to the double doors and opens them. A small crowd of people with wide smiles on their faces start to approach me, and already I feel a sense of unease. I take another deep breath, wondering if the smile I initially had is gone entirely. I force one back on my face as the first person walks up to me with a copy of my book in her hand.

"I loved this book!" the young woman says. She brushes her hair over her shoulder and her smile widens. Thankfully it's an inviting one and my uneasiness fades a little.

"Thanks so much," I tell her. "What's your name?"

"Heather," she answers and hands me the book.

I take it from her and scribble my name in it, personalized with a small message for her. I've yet to perfect an author signature. I have a few signed copies from some of my favorite authors as well and they're so pretty compared to the monstrosity I just scrawled in her book. Despite that, she smiles and thanks me.

My first signature of the day and it went well. I was so reluctant to come here today and interact with fans, but after how that one went, I'm wondering why I've struggled.

Another woman comes up to me and again is very pleasant. She asks for a picture as well and I immediately stand up from the table and lean towards her. She takes a selfie and thanks me again. I sign her book before she leaves.

Second signing done. Even better than the first.

As I sign and make small talk with fans, I begin to let go of my tension and feel more natural. It just goes to show that things never play out as terribly as you think they will. I'm not sure what I thought would happen today, but so far, everything has gone swimmingly.

A teenage girl thanks me after I sign her copy. She has such a beautiful smile and the aura around her is pure happiness to be near me. It truly melts my heart knowing that she's this way because of something I created. She tells me she's a writer herself and hopes to be like me some day.

I love knowing that I've inspired a young reader and writer like her.

Next is someone I recognize from the event. The man with the Hawaiian shirt. He smiles at me as I give a thin one back myself.

"I know I said this before," he says, "but I really

am your biggest fan." I take a deep breath when he says those words again. It irked me at the event when he did, and I tried to play it off. It's harder to do now when he's standing in front of me and repeating it. "Are you okay?" he asks.

I catch myself in my thoughts and give a wide smile. "Sorry, I must admit I'm very tired. Long day. Thank you for your question at the event, and for reading my book." He hands me a book to sign and I sigh when I look at the cover depicting the back of a young girl on a swing at night. "*The Girl I Knew*," I say. "I didn't even know you could buy a copy of this book anymore."

"They don't sell it anymore at stores or online," the man confirms. "I had to scour the net to find a copy. After I read *My Life as a Killer*, I had to buy everything you wrote. That book was my favourite, though. It was such a page-turning thriller. I've never read anything like it. A whole book from the antagonist's viewpoint. It was astounding. I never thought I'd feel so much empathy for a terrible character."

I smile, this time genuinely. "Thanks. It was something I always wanted to write. It wasn't picked up by a publisher for a long time, and for obvious reasons."

He laughs. "Not exactly your typical main character. I loved it!"

I ask for his name and sign the book, taking a moment to look at my cover. It was the first book I wrote. I remember thinking it would move worlds for me after it was published. It made a few dollars, but it was nothing like what I thought a published author would make.

Then I wrote *My Life as a Killer* and made much more than I thought I ever could from writing.

I hand the book to the man, who's ecstatic. "Anyway,

can I get a picture?" he asks, taking out his cell.

I nod. "For my number one fan, anything." I stand up from the table and he leans back beside me as he aims the camera. Before taking the picture, he wraps his arm around my shoulder. I try to hide the sensation of fear, worrying he caught my expression in the photo.

I'd prefer he didn't touch me. I'd prefer not to be here entirely. My hand begins to tremble. I grab it and hold it tightly, taking a deep breath, and try to manage my emotions.

He thanks me profusely as he leaves. I watch him as he does, and for a moment, he looks back at me, his smile growing wider before leaving through the double doors.

I wonder, is the Hawaiian shirt guy the one who ruined my life? Will I ever discover who it was?

I take a deep breath before signing the next book.

CHAPTER 3

I thank the people running the show before I leave. The hotel I'm staying at is connected to the hall and it's only a few minutes before I'll be back in my room. I sigh with relief knowing this day is over.

I've never been an extroverted person. The idea of doing what I did today is exhausting. After my presentation and book signing, all I want to do is take a nap and hibernate in my room. No doubt Matt will be out. Since coming to Toronto, he's been such a tourist. He's been travelling around all week, taking in the sights and the many things the city has to offer.

We don't do much in Chestermere. I'm a homebody by nature. He's the opposite. He's always trying to get me to go places, and usually I reluctantly agree to come with him.

I was so happy when Matt took time off from work to come to the convention with me. He knew how nervous I was. I assumed that meant he would be there to support me today for my event.

I was upset when he wasn't there. He knew how anxious I was about doing it. He knew how concerned I was about the signing. About being around fans. I was hoping he would be nearby, just to at least have his presence there. Help make me feel a little more comfortable.

I wonder what could have been more important.

As I enter the hotel lobby, a woman in her twenties smiles at me. It's an expression I'm getting used to since arriving at the convention. Recognition.

"Oh my god!" she shouts. "You're Sidney Meyers. Can I have an autograph?" She takes a step towards me. "I'm your biggest fan."

I'm not sure what it is about her. The enthusiasm in her face seems genuine enough. She seems innocent and harmless as well. But I immediately flinch as she gets closer to me. Without saying a word, I scurry past her and head towards the elevator. I press the button, but no doors open for me. I breathe in deep and look back at the young fan, who's staring at me.

She's probably thinking the same thing I am. What's wrong with you? I take another deep breath and, too impatient for the elevator to arrive, instead take the stairs. I'm only on the fourth floor. If it wasn't for my heels, it wouldn't be difficult at all to climb.

My shoes echo in the empty stairwell. I try to calm myself, wondering why I freaked out that way. She was probably just another fan, yet I reacted like she was a maniac.

This was what I feared I would be like today. I was worried I'd clam up like a scared turtle and implode on stage. When that didn't happen, I literally thought I'd explode at the book signing.

I was scared the entire time being around people. I thought maybe I would just walk off at the slightest fear. Ditch the event. Readers would see the real me.

I used to love interacting with fans. My book was a hit right from the weekend it was published. I knew my life would change; I just never thought it would be for the worse.

At the beginning, I would reply to every fan's email or post about me on Facebook. I was so thankful that they loved my writing to the point that they wanted to reach out to me.

As I get to the second floor, the stairwell door on the first floor opens and slams closed. I hear footsteps coming up. My breathing quickens as I hurry up the stairs.

I used to love interacting with fans. I used to love being a writer. The truth is, I haven't written a word in a very long time. I knew that notoriety came with its downfalls. I never suspected it would impact me like this.

The footsteps coming up the stairs start to quicken as well, and my heart beats faster. As much as my heels will allow, I run to the third-floor door and open it. I don't care that my room is on the fourth. I can't be in this stairwell.

When I'm on the third floor, I close the door behind me and don't look back as I hurry down the hallway. I have no clue where I'm going.

Suddenly I hear the stairwell door open and a man in a suit comes out, walking down the opposite hallway from me. I take another deep breath and lower my head.

I never used to be like this. Scared. I'm not even sure what I'm afraid of.

Everything changed when I received that first of many emails from one reader. The header read, "I'm your biggest fan". I clicked on the email from someone named IWriteAlone2009. It was from a Gmail account. The fan went into how much they loved *My Life as a Killer*. They went over some of their favorite scenes of the book, which for them was the graphic ways people were murdered. It put me off. It wasn't the first email like this

I'd received, though. The writer of the email never named themselves anything other than IWriteAlone2009. At the bottom of the email, they wrote: "From your number one fan."

I wondered who they were. I imagined a creative young woman who must feel very lonely. Writing can be a very isolating occupation. You're not typically around people. Was 2009 an indication of how old they were or just random numbers?

I replied back how I usually do, thanking them for reading and saying how happy I was that they liked my story. Soon after, though, I received another email from my number one fan.

It started innocently enough. IWriteAlone told me how much they enjoyed some of my other books as well. They let me know how they would buy all the rest of my books and anything I wrote in the future. A few days later, they emailed me again with praise of how they enjoyed some of my older books.

Then it started to get more personal, which I was okay with. IWriteAlone started asking me questions about my writing process and how I get into the mindset to think of the ideas I have. I answered them all, and promptly as well. I loved answering questions like this from fans. IWriteAlone said they wanted to become a writer like me, and I loved the idea that maybe I could inspire them to take a chance on their creativity.

It didn't go that way.

First, the aura of the emails changed. IWriteAlone started expressing more and more self-loathing at how they were not a published author, and I was. They put themselves down continuously and made fun of their inability to write a story. IWriteAlone said they weren't good enough to be like me.

I tried to reassure her that it was okay to feel this way. I say *her*, even though they never shared their name, gender or anything personal about themselves. I assumed it was a young woman based on what she wrote, but I never confirmed it.

One of the emails from IWriteAlone said she would "kill" to be like me, and that I should be "thankful every day" that I wasn't like her. This time I didn't reply back. There was something ominous about the email. Context matters. Perhaps she hadn't meant to come off the way she had. It's hard to tell when it's in an email.

To me, what she wrote was concerning at the least. If she was a friend, I'd have gone to her house to check on her. I didn't know anything about IWriteAlone, though, my number one fan.

I thought about asking her for more personal details. Where did she live? What was her first name? Something that I could use to confirm more about who she might be. By this time, I had already received well over thirty emails within a few weeks. I was concerned. I worried that the self loathing and hatred she seemed to have for herself could turn into self-harm.

I didn't reply to her email, though.

I was going on a trip with Matt for the week. We wanted to celebrate the success of *My Life as a Killer* by going to this resort in the Rocky Mountains. Matt made me promise him to not take my phone or laptop with me on the trip. I had to, though. I had tasks I needed to complete, even if I was on vacation.

He was getting more and more upset about me and how much time I was spending on my work as an author. I knew even back then that he was somewhat resentful of me pushing back the wedding, but as he told me, this was a once in a lifetime opportunity. I had to make the best of it I could.

When we came back from our vacation, I had many emails waiting for my reply. Emails that still make me cringe when I think of them today. Some were from my publisher and fans; I had a few regulars who would email me frequently. I enjoyed speaking with fans. I didn't have coworkers anymore. It was as if these readers had become them.

Those didn't bother me. I usually looked forward to replying to them. What did were the multiple emails from IWriteAlone. How many emails can one person send in a week? The answer: forty-one. I counted.

The oldest was harmless enough. "Hey," IWriteAlone wrote, "I just finished another of your books! Now I've read them all! You need to write more so I have something to do. Sincerely, your number one fan."

The next was written with a much different tone. "Why haven't you replied to me!" the email header read. When I clicked on it, IWriteAlone said how they took the time to write to me and was upset when I didn't reply.

I should have put on an out of office reply so that anyone who wrote while I was away would have received an email that I was gone until a certain date. I sometimes wonder what would have happened if I did. Could I have avoided everything that came after?

The email that followed was written in all capital letters. "I HATE YOU!" The email had several swearwords sprinkled in. The self-loathing she had for herself was beginning to turn to anger and rage towards me.

The emails after seemed to all have the same tone, each in all capitals. "YOU SHOULD TREAT YOUR FANS

BETTER THAN THIS!" "I DON'T DESERVE THIS!" "I WISH
YOU NOTHING BUT THE WORST!"

Made in the USA
Las Vegas, NV
01 February 2025

17367594R00156